D0455562

It's a Mystery, Pig Face!

It's a Mystery, Pig Face!

Wendy McLeod MacKnight

Sky Pony Press
New York

First Edition

This is a work of fiction. Names, characters, places, and incidents are from the author's imagination and used fictitiously.

Sky Pony Press books may be purchased in bulk at special discounts for sales promotion, corporate gifts, fund-raising, or educational purposes. Special editions can also be created to specifications. For details, contact the Special Sales Department, Sky Pony Press, 307 West 36th Street, 11th Floor, New York, NY 10018 or info@skyhorsepublishing. com.

Sky Pony® is a registered trademark of Skyhorse Publishing, Inc.®, a Delaware corporation.

Visit our website at www.skyponypress.com
Books, authors, and more at www.skyponypressblog.com

www.wendymcleodmacknight.com

10 9 8 7 6 5 4 3 2 1

Library of Congress Cataloging-in-Publication Data available on file.

Jacket image © Valerio Fabrizzi
Jacket design by Georgia Morrissey

Hardcover ISBN: 978-1-5107-0621-7
Ebook ISBN: 978-1-5107-0625-5

Printed in the United States of America

For my family, whom I love
For St. Stephen, which is always home

CHAPTER 1

Mom promised that our two-week vacation at the beach would be relaxing. She said we'd swim like dolphins, eat lobster every day, gather seashells, and tell ghost stories around the campfire. And maybe all that would have happened, except Mom forgot the one important detail that derailed everything: she forgot we were bringing my annoying little brother, Lester, a.k.a. Pig Face.

Lester being annoying was a problem, but it wasn't our biggest one. It turns out, Pig Face is allergic to the seashore. In my opinion, we should have discovered this fact before we took him to the beach for two weeks. It's not like my parents didn't know Lester had allergies.

But in the excitement of planning the trip, they forgot how nervous he gets in new places and situations and how that makes his allergies worse. The fact that he broke out in hives when he packed his suitcase should have been their first clue.

Old Orchard Beach was a Pig Face disaster: the salty air bothered his asthma, the seaweed made him itch, looking at the ocean made him woozy, and sitting around a campfire at night made him worry that the sparks would set his clothes on fire. So no, we didn't do all the fun stuff Mom promised. And that was bad, but not horrible. What ruined my vacation was that Lester decided the only way he'd survive was to stick to me like glue. For fourteen long days.

There was no place to hide. I'd wake up every morning to his saucerlike eyes staring at me, and then he'd ask if I was awake and wanted to play cards. Or he'd hear me in the bathroom and stand outside the door reading from his favorite book, *How Stuff Works*. Like anyone cares how engines work. Sometimes, I'd be so desperate for a Pig Face break, I'd sneak away to hang out with the older kids whose parents were also renting cottages at Old Orchard Beach. No matter where I went, Pig Face would always find me. He'd magically appear carrying a book he'd found in the cottage, *Eastern Coastal Birds*, in one hand, juggling his inhaler and a fly swatter in the other, and pretend to be surprised that he'd run into me.

At night (thanks to Mom and Dad's horrible idea to rent a cottage without a TV) we played games, and every night, Pig Face beat me. He'd cackle as he did a fancy Chinese checkers jump, then refuse to give me back my marbles, announcing they were now his hostages. When we played Scrabble he'd come up with bizarre—but real—words that no nine-year-old boy should know. (Who knew *pneumatic* was even a word? Pig Face.)

But the worst thing? Listening to the nonstop nose blowing. It turns out that when you're allergic to the seashore and that's where you go for two weeks, there's going to be a lot of mucus. Pig Face was a mucus-making machine.

And after two long weeks, we were mere blocks from home after an unbearable car drive full of sniffling and endless games of I Spy in which Lester seemed able to only spy my clothing or his own. I looked down at my new T-shirt, the one with VISIT OLD ORCHARD BEACH, MAINE! written across the front in big old-fashioned letters. The blue water in the picture was covered in Pig Face snot, his glistening slime making the water appear to shimmer.

Gross.

"Pig Face!"

"I can't help it," he whined. "It's my allergies. It's not my fault!"

I glared at my skinny, freckled traveling companion and noticed that not one drop of the sneeze had landed on him. *Figures.*

"Sneeze on yourself next time! Look at me: I'm covered in Pig Face goo!"

Lester grinned, which only made me more annoyed.

Mom tossed a handful of Kleenex into the backseat. "Tracy Alice Munroe—no name-calling, please and thank you. I'm sure Lester is sorry. I know it's disgusting, but a few dabs with the Kleenex and it should come right off."

A few dabs? I'm going to have to de-Lester this shirt, I thought. As I wiped myself down, I tried to focus on the happy times he and I had shared over the past couple of weeks. How he'd always backed me up when I'd dreamed up some new and elaborate activity for us and the other cottage kids to try, even if he was scared. (Who knew you could get trapped on a sandbar? Luckily, Lester had been too scared to go out in the water and had hollered for help.) How he'd let me talk for hours about my plans to become the most famous person in the history of Canada, even if I wasn't sure yet what I'd be famous for.

But for every happy memory, there was a horrible one. Like the hideous night at the fancy restaurant when he announced to the waiter that Mom and I had gone shopping for my first training bra! I can *never, ever* go back to that restaurant for as long as I live.

The awful memories made me dab harder until I'd completely destroyed the Kleenex. I looked up. Pig Face was trying not to laugh at my goo-removal technique, but he wasn't doing a very good job, making strange *rat-tat-tat* sounds like a strangled woodpecker. Looking down at the soggy mess in my hand, I thought about tossing it at him, but then noticed Mom staring at me in the rearview mirror as though she'd read my mind.

I dutifully tossed the wad into a small garbage bag and gave Lester my best *you'll pay for this* look.

"Look—there's Carman's Diner!" Lester called out.

His diversionary tactic worked. The flashing neon Carman's Diner sign was like a beacon for the home-sick; it meant we were only two blocks from home. Home: our dog Charlie, our friends, our own beds, and the rest of the summer. The Maine seashore had been fun, but the little town of St. Stephen? It was the best, at least as far as I was concerned.

I rolled down the window and stuck my head out. "I can smell the chocolate factory!"

"Me too!" Lester cried, doing the same thing.

"Your nose hasn't been unstuffed in two weeks, Pig Face. You couldn't smell a chocolate bar if it was right under your schnozzle!"

Actually, I couldn't smell chocolate, either, but I always liked to think I could. The Ganong factory was only a couple of blocks from our house, a Wonka-like brick building dedicated to all things worth living for—chocolates, peppermints, and gummies.

"Tracy, his name is Lester," said the warning voice from the front seat.

"Sorry, Lester, dear." I leaned over and tweaked one of his dimples just like Aunt Gladys always does. I knew it drove him batty. Lester seemed ready to file an official protest when the car rounded the corner onto Marks Street.

Dad was creeping along, enjoying reconnecting with the neighborhood: "Peter hasn't cut his lawn since we left town! Millidge and Julie got a new car!" We passed a boy I'd never seen before walking on the side of the road. He turned slightly, as if he thought we were stalking him, hardly surprising since Dad was driving so slowly.

I couldn't get a good look at the kid's face. *I wonder if he's staying around here*, I thought, but the thought vanished as we pulled into the driveway.

Seeing Ralph Huffman sitting on my doorstep was like seeing an oasis after a desert of Pig Face. I'd texted Ralph an hour before, and there he and Charlie were: my two most faithful friends, waiting. Charlie had bunked with Ralph while we were away, and from the way she was half-sitting on his lap, it seemed that being roomies had suited them both. As soon as they saw the car they were on their feet. It was hard to tell which of them was more excited. Ralph let the leash go as we opened our doors and Charlie bounded forward, yelping with happiness. Now my damp T-shirt had a layer of Charlie slobber and kisses added to it. But you couldn't be upset about *that*. That was love.

"How are you?" I gasped at Ralph when I finally disentangled myself from a writhing Charlie.

"I'm good now," he said, grabbing a suitcase from my dad, "but it was so boring with you out of town. Plus, everyone else I know was away, too, so I was stuck hanging out with Willie. We watched *baseball*," he added, his face scrunching up like he'd just sucked on a lemon.

Willie is Ralph's brother. He's a year younger than us—he just turned ten—and he and Ralph are so unalike you'd think they were born on different planets.

"So—are you a baseball fan now?" I asked, poking Ralph in the side with my elbow as we walked into my house. Inside the kitchen, I took a big breath; it still smelled like home.

Ralph set down the suitcase and pretended to throw a ball. "He made me do this with him after supper. Every. Single. Day. It was horrible. At least after the first couple days he stopped saying I throw like a girl."

"Hey! You tell Willie that's insulting! I throw pretty good!"

"You do not, Tracy. You're as bad a thrower as I am. Anyway, when he wasn't making me play ball with him, he'd sit and watch sports on TV for hours. One afternoon, he even watched cricket 'cause that was the only thing on TV. Have you ever *watched* cricket?"

I shook my head. I wasn't sure I knew what cricket was.

"Trust me, you're not missing much. The only bright spot was that he never gave me a hard time when I wanted to watch the Food Network. He likes food too much. Mostly, we just sat around staring at each other. But it's okay now. You're back, and this morning Willie left for hockey camp for two weeks. I feel like summer is finally starting."

"Poor you. Don't worry. I'll think of all kinds of cool stuff for us to do for the rest of the summer."

"I knew I could count on you." Ralph's smile was so wide it was practically splitting his face in two. I usually only saw Ralph that happy after he'd mastered a difficult culinary technique, like making a perfect flaky piecrust. He must have been really bored spending so much time with Willie.

We stopped briefly in my room so I could give Ralph the gifts I'd bought for him. I have to admit, I'm pretty much the best souvenir shopper in the world. I am not the best packer, however, and I began to paw through my messy suitcase, tossing dirty clothes and flip-flops behind me, looking for his presents.

"Hey! That's my head you know," Ralph sputtered as a sandal caught his ear on its way to join its mate on the floor.

"Sorry."

"You always say you're sorry," Ralph said, "but are you *really* sorry?"

I giggled. "I'm *kind* of sorry. . . ."

I seemed to have brought most of Old Orchard Beach home with me; everything in the suitcase was covered in a salty-smelling grit that reminded me of the hours spent exploring the shoreline. After tossing aside yet another pair of flip-flops and hauling out a large bag of seashells, I found gift number one.

"What do you think?" I asked, handing Ralph the dried carcass of a crab.

"Cool," he said. "But it kind of stinks, doesn't it?"

Leaning over, I took a good long sniff. It did smell a little strong. "It just needs to be aired out and then it won't smell at all. I like the aroma. It's like I've brought you a little of the ocean."

Ralph nodded, but it was clear he didn't share my belief that airing it out would do the trick.

"Maybe you could cook it," I suggested.

"You do know about health codes and the risk of eating dead stuff off the beach, don't you?"

I shrugged. "No, but then I'm not the one who's going to be the Michelin Star Chef someday, am I?" Even though I don't know what a Michelin Star Chef is, I know it's a big deal and that Ralph is going to be one, and that's good enough for me. I imagined big glittery stars all over his restaurant's menu drawn by *moi*.

"Thank goodness." Ralph placed the crab on my windowsill.

I ignored the remark and returned my attention to my nearly empty suitcase. Balled in a side pocket was gift number two, the one I'd actually paid for. It was a T-shirt, but not a touristy one like I was wearing. It was cool, with a picture of the cover of Ralph's favorite book, *A Wrinkle in Time*, on the front. Mom and I couldn't believe it when I spotted it in one of the funky stores near the beach.

"That's what I'm talking about!" Ralph put the shirt right on and looked in the mirror. "I love it!"

The T-shirt was a men's large, the same size my dad wears. Ralph is the tallest boy in St. Stephen Elementary School and will probably be the tallest boy when we get to middle school in the fall. Unless something dramatic happened over the summer, I was for sure going to be the shortest girl. We get a lot of stupid comments and jokes about our height difference and believe me, none of them are funny. I keep hoping for a growth spurt—I'm only eleven, after all—but whenever I ask Dr. Fingard about the possibility of becoming a giantess, he just points at Mom, who is the shortest lady I know. Since receiving this heartbreaking news, I've done ten minutes of stretching every night before bed and ten minutes of hanging upside down on the monkey bars every afternoon in the desperate hope that my bones will lengthen. You never know—it might work. And then I'll be a gazillionaire because I'll sell my bone-lengthening secret to short people everywhere.

While Ralph continued to admire himself in the mirror, I finished emptying my suitcase. One of the last things I pulled out was a small wind-up Ferris wheel. I sighed and placed it on my dresser. It sat there mocking me, so I decided to stick it in my top drawer instead.

Curious, Ralph opened the drawer and pulled the Ferris wheel back out. "Did you buy this in Old Orchard Beach?" Before I could respond, he wound it up, and we watched as the wheel went around five or six times, making a slight metallic clanging sound with each rotation.

I grimaced. "I didn't buy it; my dad did. It's his idea of a joke. He bought it for me after I went on the Ferris wheel at the amusement park."

"No way—you're terrified of heights! Why would you go on a Ferris wheel?"

. There was a loud snort behind us. Lester stood in the doorway, ready to pounce. "Pig Face . . ." My tone was a warning shot, but I knew he'd tell the story anyway. It was too good not to share. Even *I* would've told the story, only I would've changed it so the main character's name wasn't Tracy, but something dull, like Mildred.

Ralph shoved the suitcase aside and sat down on my bed. "What happened?" He'd seen the pained look on my face and was expecting maximum entertainment value.

Pig Face took a deep breath, pleased to have Ralph's undivided attention. "You know how Tracy's scared of heights, right?"

Ralph rolled his eyes. "I just said that. *Everyone* knows she's scared of heights. Go on."

"Okay, so Mom and Dad took us to the amusement

park a few days after we got to Old Orchard Beach. Dad and I immediately got in line for the Ferris wheel, while Tracy and Mom waited near where you get on and off the ride."

"I'm surprised you wanted to go on a Ferris wheel, too," Ralph said. "You're not exactly brave yourself, Lester."

I could see Lester bristle. He wasn't afraid of amusement park rides or heights and was very proud of that fact. I could see the wheels in his little Pig Face brain whirring. Should he say something smart to Ralph or let it go? In the end, he continued with the agonizing story of the Ferris wheel and me.

"The guy running the controls kept teasing Tracy, saying stuff like 'Don't you feel funny that your little brother is going on and you aren't?' That kind of thing. She tried to ignore him, but he wouldn't stop. Mom kept telling her he was only teasing, but I could tell it was bugging Tracy."

I began to chew at the cuticle of my right thumb. "It was embarrassing."

Ralph raised an eyebrow. "I get that you were

embarrassed, but I still don't get why you went on the ride."

"It was *his* fault," I said, pointing at Pig Face. "Lester's not telling the whole story. The guy running the ride wasn't the only person giving me a hard time. Lester started telling everybody in line about how scared I am of heights and how he isn't. I got mad."

Ralph grinned at Lester. "You really got to her, huh?"

Lester giggled. "Uh-huh! She *begged* to go on. Mom kept telling her it was a bad idea, but you know what she's like when she gets something into her head."

"Won't take no for an answer."

Lester nodded. "It was fine on the way up . . ."

My stomach lurched. I chewed harder.

"But then we got close to the top and the guy stopped the wheel a couple of times to let more people on and off. The motion of the wheel stopping and then starting again made all the seats start to rock. That's when things turned ugly."

"Did you throw up?" Ralph asked me. I shook my head.

Lester snorted, which in turn made him need to

blow his nose. He did so, loudly, and then continued my tale of woe. "Throwing up would have been
better. She screamed bloody murder. Then the Ferris
wheel moved again and when it started to go faster,
Tracy screamed louder. When she whizzed by the guy
at the controls she yelled 'GET ME OFF!' in a deep
creepy voice, like she was possessed by demons. It was
so funny! But the guy couldn't stop the ride right away,
so she and Mom went up and over again, with Tracy
screaming the whole way. When she finally got off I
could tell the guy felt bad. He patted her on the head
and said 'There, there, little girl' like she was four years
old."

"It was horrible." I shuddered. I could still picture the look the guy had given me as he unlatched
the safety bar; it made me feel like a little kid. Even
worse, my screaming had drawn a crowd. It was like I'd
become the newest carnival attraction, and everyone
was either laughing or looking at me with pity. "It's the
worst thing that's ever happened to me. I was so sure I
had outgrown my fear of heights."

Ralph laughed and then got to his feet. "Clearly you

didn't. But you know better than to let Lester get to you like that."

I glanced down at my cuticle, which looked like it had been mangled by a wild creature. "I know. It was weird. Like spending all that time with him made me lose my anti–Pig Face defense system."

"Don't worry. You'll get it back soon enough. C'mon. Let's go for a walk, just the *two* of us." Ralph emphasized the word *two* for Lester's benefit, since my little mucus-maker seemed ready to grab his sneakers and come along. "I've got stories, though none as exciting as yours. The big one is this: a guy our age just moved in next door."

I chose a floppy sun hat from the rack that held St. Stephen's best hat collection, stuck my tongue out at Lester, who did likewise back to me, and followed Ralph out my bedroom door, making a pit stop at the bathroom for a Band-Aid for my poor finger. Lester didn't make the cut to go with us, but Charlie did, so I attached the leash to her collar, told Mom we were going for a walk, and the three of us stepped out the front door. I took a deep breath and smiled. It felt good to be back in my own neighborhood, free to wander around without Mom and Dad breathing down my neck or Lester stalking me like in Old Orchard Beach.

"So tell me about this guy," I said as we headed down the front walk. "Is he nice?"

"He's the most obnoxious guy I've ever met. You're going to hate his guts."

CHAPTER 2

We'd only made it as far as the house next door when Charlie needed a pit stop.

"So what's the story on this guy you think is so obnoxious?" I asked as I reached into my pocket for a plastic bag.

"Hazel McNutt's rented her basement apartment to him and his father," Ralph said, nodding in the direction of the house in front of us. "They're from New York City and they're in town for July and August. You left on your trip on July first, right? I think they came on July third. The dad's working on something with the new bridge the town's building."

"What makes the guy so obnoxious? You and I love

New York City. I'm surprised that isn't enough to make you like him."

Ralph and I dreamed of moving to New York City when we grew up. Of course, neither of us had ever been to New York City, but if it was anything like the movies, it would be perfect for Ralph's career as a chef and my career doing something that would make me famous. As I waited for Ralph's response, I gave a sneaky glance at Charlie. She won't go if you watch her.

"I may love New York City, but I don't love him. I met him a couple of days after they arrived." Ralph looked grim. "He's thirteen, and all he talked about was New York City this, New York City that, how small and boring St. Stephen is, how he hasn't met anybody interesting."

I couldn't imagine anyone thinking Ralph wasn't interesting. Still waiting on Charlie, I glanced at Hazel's garden and saw that she'd gotten a new gnome while we were gone. This one was perched kind of awkwardly on a red and white polka-dot mushroom, like he was posing in a magazine. Like everything else about Hazel, it was creepy.

"He looks like the type who buys all his clothes at trendy stores. You should have seen his sneakers—they're superexpensive. And wait till you see how Jasmine Singh acts around him. It's like he's the first guy she's ever seen before." Ralph pretended to dry heave, much to my delight.

"Gross," I said. In my mind I was already wondering how furious Jasmine was that this new guy was living next door to me for the summer. I bet she was fuming.

Jasmine Singh is almost everything I'm not. She has long black hair that hangs in perfectly straight lines down to her waist, the polar opposite of my wild curls. Her skin is this beautiful caramel color; mine is half pasty-white and half boiled lobster. She's tall, and I'm notoriously short. The only thing we have in common is that we're both good students. It seems like we're always competing for the best grades. A long time ago, in kindergarten, Jasmine and I were good friends. But then I humiliated her when I accidentally tripped her and she flashed her *Dora the Explorer* underwear to the whole class. She refused to forgive me and it's been downhill ever since.

I continued on my quirky path and she took the road most traveled, joining the ranks of the girls who giggle nonstop about everything. Now it seems like everything is a competition between us. And when we weren't competing at school, her favorite activity was trying to torture me.

Ralph and I were definitely *not* trendy. We wore secondhand clothes to save the environment, and so we wouldn't look like everyone else at school. Our classmates patrolled the malls; we hit yard sales. Thanks to my grandpa, Ralph and I were fans of old black-and-white movies. My walls were plastered with pictures of Audrey Hepburn, Fred Astaire, and Humphrey Bogart, while Ralph's were covered in pictures of John Wayne and famous chefs like Gordon Ramsay.

Thank goodness Ralph and I had found each other in kindergarten. I was the one wearing the wild hat covered in plastic cherries and sporting fancy white gloves. Ralph had chosen polka-dot suspenders. We took one look at each other across a sea of small wooden desks and sand tables and knew we were—like Anne of Green Gables always says—kindred spirits. We've been inseparable ever since. The one thing Ralph and I can't agree on is music; he likes head-banger stuff from the 1980s and rap, while I'm obsessed with 1970s disco, Bing Crosby, and Frank Sinatra. We've agreed to disagree.

Charlie was finally done. Just as I was about to lean over and pick up the present she'd left behind, Hazel's screen door flew open. Out stepped my archenemy, Jasmine, followed immediately by her aunt, the beast that was Hazel McNutt.

"Tracy Munroe!" Hazel hollered. "You keep your dog off my grass!"

Before I could defend myself, Hazel smiled at Ralph. "How are you, Ralph?"

Confused by Hazel's sudden friendliness, I stood frozen, doggy bag in hand.

"Don't just stand there, Tracy. Clean it up!" Hazel barked.

This set Jasmine into a fit of giggles, which made me seriously consider leaving Charlie's gift for Hazel to deal with. I watched in disgust as she smirked and walked down the driveway, teetering on her high heels, acting like she was walking the runway in some beauty pageant. As Jasmine passed us, she reached up and held her nose as if Ralph and I smelled as bad as what I was about to put in the doggy bag. Then she scurried away down the street, a rat in red-and-purple leggings.

Ralph crossed his eyes at me and I giggled, which seemed to set Hazel off again.

"You be careful, Ralph. You don't want Tracy to get you in trouble."

Ralph's eyes uncrossed and he gave Hazel a slight nod. For some reason, her comment made Ralph nervous. I didn't like it. I laughed again, knowing that would bother Hazel.

"Don't you laugh at me, Tracy Munroe. I just had a man fertilize that grass!"

Hazel pointed to a small sign nearby that I hadn't noticed. Her purple sequined top sparkled in the light and her teased orange hair bounced like a fluffy pumpkin stuck to the top of her head as she continued pointing and shaking her head. It was magnificent in a horrible-but-mesmerizing kind of way.

Hazel McNutt hated me. Actually, Hazel McNutt hated *everyone*, except maybe Jasmine, whom she invited over from time to time to admire her new stuff. She especially hated everyone since her husband left her three years ago on the day before her fiftieth birthday. Mom said that made Hazel's ex-husband lowdown and mean, but she also said it was a big secret, so we could never talk about it in public. I'd protested that everybody in town already knew what Mr. McNutt did, but Mom said that didn't matter, which made absolutely no sense to me. Now that she didn't have a husband, all Hazel did was shop online and read romance novels, and the only men in her life were the UPS guys who brought her packages twice a week.

"Okay, Mrs. McNutt," I said, tying off the Charlie bag. "We're going." Under my breath I whispered to

Ralph, "I hope this fertilizer is organic. She'll be talking to my lawyer if you or Charlie or I grow extra arms."

"You don't have a lawyer," Ralph reminded me. I shrugged, grabbed his arm, and yanked on Charlie's leash. We walked away, and I was pleased with myself for surviving another run-in with Hurricane Hazel.

"I'm watching you, Tracy Munroe!" Hazel shouted after me. *Whatever*, I thought. *I'm watching you, too, Hazel McNutt.*

We were almost past my driveway when a voice I didn't recognize called out my name.

Ralph muttered, "It's the New York guy," under his breath as we turned.

Walking toward us was the best-looking boy I'd ever seen: all floppy hair, baggy T-shirt, skinny jeans, and Vans sneakers. A ball cap was tucked artfully in his back pocket, like he'd stepped out of a teen movie. I couldn't help but notice how hypnotic his green eyes were and how his eyebrows had just the right amount of bushiness.

Glancing sideways at Ralph, I could tell he was completely unimpressed. I gave myself a shake; if Ralph was unimpressed, well, so was I. Still, as I watched the New York boy come toward us, moving like he was in a slow-motion video, I couldn't help wishing that there wasn't dried snot on my T-shirt and that Ralph liked this guy, at least a little.

"You must be Tracy," the boy-band clone said. "I'm Zach Favola. I'm staying next door. I've been waiting for you and your brother to get home. Hazel told me all about you. She said I'd know it was you when I saw a head full of wild red hair." He smiled, and I could almost count every one of his perfectly straight teeth. I intended to give him the cold shoulder, but I could feel his charms start to work on me. I thought of the red curls that did their own thing regardless of what I tried to tame them, and reached up to touch them self-consciously. Then something snapped and I gave my head a shake. I was not going to be one of those girls who got all silly over a pretty face.

When I didn't respond right away, he continued. "I'm from New York City. I've already met Ralph a few times. How are you, man?"

"I'm good," Ralph said. "Have you had a stroke, Tracy? You're never this quiet."

Typical Ralph.

I pulled myself together, afraid that he might say something else embarrassing. "Welcome to the neighborhood," I said, pleased at how casual my voice sounded.

"Thanks," Zach said. "Maybe we can hang out sometime?"

"Tracy and I hang out a lot," Ralph said, pointedly. That was true, but kind of a weird thing for Ralph to say.

Zach smiled his dazzling smile again. Despite my determination to give this guy a wide berth, I could see why Jasmine was so taken with him. He was different from the other boys our age in St. Stephen. There was a strange glow about him, as if spotlights were shining on him. It was like meeting a movie star. "Sure, man," he said to Ralph. "Whatever. We can all hang out."

I glanced at Ralph. No way was he planning to hang

out with Zach anytime soon. "Maybe," I said, trying to keep my expression as neutral as possible. I didn't want to offend Zach—I barely knew him, after all—but I was conscious of Ralph watching me, waiting to see if I was going to fall under Zach's spell, too.

Which I definitely was not.

Even though I'd just met Zach, I could tell that my "maybe" had thrown him. He was probably used to girls throwing themselves at his feet. "Um, great," he stammered, turning to go. "I've been kind of bored. I'm glad you and your brother are home." And then, just like that, he was gone. Marks Street returned to its normal state and I gave myself a shake, kind of embarrassed.

"When you can breathe again, let's drop Charlie off at your house and take that walk," Ralph said. He jerked the leash away from me and began taking pur- poseful steps up my driveway. "Trust me: New York is not what he appears to be. Did you see what he was wearing? And I think he styles his hair."

"His name is Zach," I protested as I hurried to catch

up. "And give me a break—he's kind of dazzling, but I'm not Jasmine. Plus, he's prettier than I am!"

Ralph laughed. "Yeah, I guess he's good looking, but you can tell he knows it."

"Well, he and Jasmine can have each other," I said. Still, it was exciting that St. Stephen was suddenly home to a heartthrob, and despite my loyalty to my best friend, I couldn't help but be a little thrilled that the heartthrob had moved into the house next door.

CHAPTER 3

After dropping Charlie off and quickly changing my clothes, Ralph and I grabbed Popsicles and headed toward the baseball field. To get there, we cut through the woody grove behind my house. This was my thinking place, with plenty of bushes and trees to escape to for peace and quiet, especially when Pig Face was getting on my nerves. At the heart of the grove is a small swamp; thick masses of cattails rise like miniature skyscrapers in a prickly city, its only citizens the frogs and turtles we catch and release.

As we tramped along, careful to avoid roots and mucky puddles, Ralph filled me in on his last two weeks. Besides a couple of Willie incidents, most of his time had revolved around the Food Network or his kitchen. I got to hear all about the virtues of cream and butter and his dream of mastering the soufflé, whatever that is. But I was only half-listening; I was thinking about how exciting it was to have someone from New York City living next door to me.

Ralph stopped. He looked down at me, searching my face for clues. "Is something wrong? Usually I can't get a word in edgewise. You're not thinking about that guy are you?"

I never lied to Ralph. "Actually, I was thinking it was kind of cool that New Yorkers were living next door," I admitted.

Ralph's face puckered like he'd swallowed a lemon. He started to speak, but I held up a hand. "Wait—let me finish. I *do* think it's cool. You know I've always wanted to visit New York City."

I got a grudging nod in response, so I kept going. "But I get it. You don't like him, so that's good enough for me." I reached down and plucked a long piece of Timothy grass. I stuck the end in my mouth and began to chew, pretending I was a farmer surveying my land.

"I am so happy to be home. I love the ocean, but this is my kingdom."

Ralph grabbed his own piece of Timothy grass and motioned for me to lead the way. "It feels so weird when you're not around."

I smiled as I shoved aside a pine bough that was directly in my path. Only I kind of forgot to hold it for Ralph and it snapped back and hit him hard in the right shoulder. He yelped.

"You gotta hold them!" Ralph snapped. "You know the rule."

I pretended to look sorry. It was impossible to count the number of times a pine bough had hit me in the face when Ralph was breaking the trail, which is why we'd made the "hold the branch" rule to begin with. After that I'd been more careful, although I refused to acknowledge the dramatic way Ralph was rubbing his shoulder. We stepped out of the grove and onto the baseball field.

"Weird," Ralph said, glancing around. "Hardly anyone's here."

In the distance we could see a guy running the

track. I couldn't see his face, but he was long and lanky and wearing a red T-shirt and shorts. I was pretty sure it was Joe Tunney, our paperboy. Exiting the field at the farthest point from where we stood were Jasmine and a couple of her friends. I was impressed she'd made it over to the field so quickly in her stupid high heels, and relieved that we'd missed her and her pack. There'd be doggy-doo jokes the next time I ran into her; I was certain of it.

Ralph pointed toward the receding backs of the Plastic Posse. I'd given them the nickname in third grade because they reminded me of the little painted plastic dolls I played with. The name had stuck.

"Here's something that will make you doubly happy you were on vacation: Jasmine was staying with Hazel last week while her parents were out of town."

I made a gagging sound. About once a year, Jasmine stayed with Hazel for a while. I'd come out the front door and there she'd be, sitting on a lawn chair in Hazel's yard. The hedge that separated our property from Hazel's would feel like the No Man's Land we'd learned about in social studies—the empty piece of land dividing opposing armies in World War One that belonged to no one. Every time I went outside, I'd feel Jasmine's beady dark eyes watching me. I couldn't be comfortable in my own yard and I hated it. Ralph was right—I was doubly happy I was on vacation, even with all of Pig Face's antics.

"While you were away, she acted like she owned the neighborhood. She and Zach ran around town like they were in a movie. It would have made you sick."

Everything about Jasmine made me sick. Probably because she took every chance she got to make fun of me. If I got an answer right in class—which was almost all the time—I'd hear her muttering to anyone who'd listen about how I never let anyone else have a chance. In gym class, she'd make fun of the eczema on my legs—"Do you have a horrible disease, Tracy?"—or about the fact that I could almost never sink a basket because of my height. I wasn't the only kid in school Jasmine tortured, but I was her favorite target, probably because I fought back. The idea of the most horrible girl I knew hanging out with Mr. Movie Star New York City definitely made me feel sick. I was supposed to be the person living a glamorous life in St. Stephen! I blotted the image out of my mind. Instead, I pictured myself decked out in big sunglasses and an enormous straw hat, window-shopping with Zach downtown. I could see everyone whispering about us, wondering who he was and when I'd become so fabulous. I adjusted my hat and allowed the glamour to wash over me.

My dream sequence was brief. The midday sun and my imagination were making me feel warm—too warm. I needed some shade, stat. "C'mon, let's go sit in one of the dugouts."

Ralph followed me to the closest one. I wrinkled my nose at the smell of wet wood; not exactly pleasant, but at least it was better than boiling in the sun.

We took a seat on the bench and slurped and crunched our way through the Popsicles.

"Hey, Ralph. We should think of some kind of project for the rest of the summer." I had the urge to do something awesome before I was sentenced back to school.

"What kind of project?"

"I don't know. Maybe something that will make us famous?"

Ralph stared off into the distance, deep in thought. All of a sudden, he got excited and turned to me. "I have an idea: you could help me conquer the soufflé. We could film me practicing, put it on the web, and get like a million hits. That would make us famous."

"Do you think a lot of people would watch you make a soufflé?" I could tell straightaway that the doubt in my voice had offended him; he'd crossed his arms and his face had gone the color of a tomato.

"Food lovers would" was his stiff reply.

Sensing I needed to be more careful with my words, I changed my tactics. "You're right; a kid making a video about mastering the soufflé would be great. But that's your project, not mine. Besides, I have my own project. I'm going to learn how to sew so I can jazz up the vintage stuff I buy from Trixie's."

Trixie's was an amazing secondhand store where I bought most of my clothing. "We can have our own projects," I said, "but we need to think of something we can do together, something we've never done before."

I watched Ralph's face. The red faded to pink and then disappeared altogether. He uncrossed his arms and waited for me to continue. "Remember last summer when we decided we'd dig a path from my yard over to the field here?" I pictured the now-overgrown path that we'd abandoned after only ten feet. Who knew digging a hundred-foot-long trail would be so hard? "I was thinking that we could do something easier this summer. And I like your idea of putting something on YouTube. Maybe we can make a movie based on one of our favorite films like *Casablanca*, post it online, and become bazillionaires."

Ralph seemed to consider this for a moment, then nodded. I knew he'd like the idea of being a bazillionaire. "It might be hard to remake *Casablanca*. Where would we get an airplane?" he asked.

He had a point. I tried to picture Ingrid Bergman walking away from Humphrey Bogart toward my swamp. It just wasn't the same. "Gotcha. Okay, let's spitball some ideas. We could do a film about crime in St. Stephen or—"

"I don't think there's much crime around town,"

Ralph interrupted. "How about we do a documentary on the secret life of Hazel McNutt? You know, we could make it all dark and creepy and twisted. We could follow her around. Film all of the weird things she does."

"The only weird things Hazel does are read romance novels and buy junk off the Internet. Who'd want to watch *that*?"

"I was in her house while you were gone," Ralph said. "It was creepy. You should see her bathroom."

"You were in her bathroom? Wait. Why were you in her bathroom?"

Ralph's face went pink again. "I was walking by her house the day after you left and she asked if I'd come in and get something down from the attic for her. She's got one of those hole-in-the-ceiling kind of attics that you need a stepladder to get into it. Apparently, Hazel's terrified of ladders."

I'd finally found the one thing Hazel and I had in common. My fear of heights made me scared to death of ladders, too.

"I was wondering why she was so nice to you when

we ran into her earlier. But why didn't she get Zach
or his dad to get it for her? They're right there in the
house."

"They hadn't moved in yet."

"Makes sense. Okay, so you went into her attic . . ."

"Yeah—she needed a box. I don't think she's been
able to get things out of the attic since Mr. McNutt
left. Anyway, I got the box for her and she was happy.
She gave me five dollars and a glass of lemonade. I had
to use her bathroom before I left, which is why I know
what it looks like."

"So . . . what does it look like?" I'd tried imagining
Hazel's house before, but I could never decide if it was
dark and sinister—like the Wicked Witch of the West's
castle—or fussy, filled with china dolls, their eerie glass
eyes watching your every move, just like Hazel always
watched mine.

"It's like someone threw up all the gold curtains,
pillows, and ruffles in the world and put them into one
house." Ralph shuddered, then closed his eyes for a
second, as if he was trying to erase the image from his
mind. I was mesmerized.

I leaned forward and gave him a poke. "And . . ."

"She has a picture of herself, holding a rose, all dramatic-like, on her bathroom wall. The picture is black and white, except for the red rose. I still have nightmares about it. The corner of her living room is full of unopened boxes. Isn't that weird? And there was a pile of expensive-looking jewelry just lying on a coffee table, like she's a queen. Hazel must have a lot of money if she can afford all that stuff and if she can buy things she doesn't even bother to open. I wouldn't mind that kind of money."

"I don't get the part about the unopened packages. When I get something in the mail, I rip it open right away."

"I don't understand, either. No one needs *that* much stuff. And it kind of made me mad. I bet my mom would love some of the jewelry Hazel has just lying around. Mom's so careful with her money, making sure Willie has the right hockey equipment or that I have what I need for cooking. She never gets to buy anything nice for herself."

"I guess the unopened packages explain all those UPS trucks," I said.

"Uh-huh. But it doesn't explain how she can afford all that stuff. Maybe our film could figure that out."

"There is no way I am making a film about Hazel McNutt. Not gonna happen." I studied my sneakers. "On the other hand, interviewing a kid from New York City who's living in St. Stephen for the summer might be interesting. We could ask him a bunch of questions so we'd know what to expect when we moved there. Plus, it would make Jasmine go ballistic."

Ralph didn't respond. I gave it a moment, then glanced up. He looked revolted. "Interviewing Zach is not gonna happen either, even if it would be a great way to stick it to Jasmine. Everything I need to know about New York City I can read online or watch in a movie."

I knew better than to argue when Ralph's voice went all prickly. He pulled a pack of gum from his shorts pocket and handed me a stick of Juicy Fruit. The quick hit of sweetness in my mouth canceled out the stale odors of the dugout. He stuffed the package of gum back into his pocket, but not before I saw him pop another stick into his own mouth. The gum wrapper slipped from his hand and fluttered to the wooden floor below us.

"Thanks for offering me another piece," I said as sarcastically as I could, leaning over to pick up his trash. I hate littering and was beginning to plan my Ralph-shaming when something golden brown under the bench caught my eye. It looked like a paper bag, but it was hard to tell for sure because it was partially covered by dirt and dried leaves.

I got down on all fours but couldn't quite reach.

"What are you doing?" Ralph leaned over to take a look.

"Someone left some garbage under here and I wanted to grab it and throw it out when I toss *your* gum wrapper."

Ralph got down on his hands and knees beside me. "I was going to pick the wrapper up, you know. You're not the only one who cares about the environment." He reached for what was, indeed, a paper bag. The top was rolled tightly so its contents wouldn't spill out. Ralph brushed off the dirt with his T-shirt, and I watched as little bits of dust and leaves rained back down on the dirt floor.

When we stood up, I held out my hand ready to throw what I assumed was just garbage into a nearby trash can.

Ralph gave the bag a little shake and handed it over. "It's heavy. Probably a rotten banana or a can of pop."

It *was* heavy. I gave the bag my own gentle shake. "I can't tell what it is. What do you think? Should we open it and take a look or just throw it out?"

Ralph recoiled. "I wouldn't open that. What if there's a severed finger or a rat inside?"

I shook the bag again. "You've been watching too many scary movies. Plus, a severed finger would ooze, wouldn't it? I say we look."

"You're going to regret opening that," Ralph said, but he took a seat beside me on the bench and watched as I began to unroll the top of the bag.

I held the bag between us. "Want to look together?"

Ralph shook his head and turned away. "Nope. If

it's gross you can just tell me about it. You know how chefs hate spoiled food."

I pulled the bag open, looked down inside, and gasped.

"You gotta see this!" I whispered.

Ralph leaned back away from me. "Is it something disgusting?"

"No—it's amazing!"

He leaned over, too curious to worry that something might jump out at him.

"It *is* amazing."

Lying in the bottom of the bag was a wad of money held together by a thick rubber band.

CHAPTER 4

I pulled out the money and removed the elastic band. The money fanned out and extended over the sides of my palm. The outer bill was a hundred dollars with the bespectacled and bemused face of Benjamin Franklin. Ben looked happy to see us. I was sure happy to see him. The fact that it was American money wasn't surprising; St. Stephen was separated from Calais, Maine, by a narrow river, and lots of people shopped over there. Most St. Stephen wallets contained at least a few American bills.

"Wow! A stack of Benjamins," Ralph said.

"Benjamins?"

Ralph pointed at Franklin. "Benjamins is slang

for hundred-dollar bills. All the rappers use it. If you weren't so busy listening to that old music you'd know this stuff."

I rolled my eyes.

I grabbed the now empty bag and examined it inside and out for a name or other distinguishing marks that could tell us who the money belonged to. There weren't any.

"This is a lot of money," I said. "Who leaves a paper bag filled with cash in a baseball dugout? Let's look through the bills, check if there's a note inside."

Ralph nudged me and nodded toward Joe, who was still running the track. "It's too public here. We should look at the money somewhere private. What if someone comes along and mugs us?"

"I doubt Joe's going to mug us. I thought you said he was a good guy?" Ralph and Joe had played on the same hockey team a couple of years ago, before Ralph realized that he hated hockey and couldn't skate worth spit.

Ralph continued to scan the horizon for potential muggers. "He is a good guy. Still . . ." I stood up to go, but Ralph clutched my arm. "Wait—are we thieves if we take it with us?"

I thought of all the mystery books I'd read and shook my head. "I don't think so, unless we keep the money, which we won't do, right?"

Ralph looked horrified. "Of course we won't!"

"Let's take the money and find a way to return it to its rightful owner. If we leave it here someone else will find it and they might keep it. We owe it to the owner to take care of it."

I imagined myself handing the money to some faceless person, them clasping me in their arms and crying tears of joy for returning the family fortune. I heard the newspaper reporter saying, "How were you so smart to figure out who'd lost the money?" I'd reply, "It was easy." We'd be heroes. Just thinking about all of the attention we'd get had me completely pumped, like there was extra energy running through my body. It was all I could do not to go run a lap with Joe.

Instead, I took a deep breath, put the money back into the bag, and handed it to Ralph to tuck into one of his pockets. "Let's go count the money in Mrs. Attwood's barn. No one will see us there."

"Who knows," Ralph said as we stepped out of the dugout. "Maybe there'll be a reward for returning the money. We could go to Hollywood. You could hang with movie stars and I could become a famous chef."

I hadn't even thought about the possibility of a reward. "Hollywood, here we come!" I whooped. After a couple of energetic high fives, Ralph and I raced off to Mrs. Attwood's barn to count the money we were both certain would lead to our fame and fortune.

Mrs. Attwood, or Mrs. A. as I like to call her, lived across the street from me. The gray-shingled barn behind her house stored a prized Model T Ford, the perfect place to sit and count the money in private. The barn door was locked when we got there, but it was no problem to jimmy one of the windows open and crawl through. We'd done it lots of times before when we were playing hide-and-seek. We climbed into the car like we were going for a Sunday drive, with me behind the wheel because Ralph said he was too nervous to drive. As soon as we were settled, he took the bag out of his pocket and pulled out the money.

"How much do you guess is in here?" he asked.

"I bet it's at least a thousand dollars."

"I say a million dollars!" He fanned his face with the money and cackled like a madman.

"Calm down, Rockefeller," I said. "I can tell it's not a million. It's mostly small bills, fives and tens."

I grabbed the money and began to count out loud, laying bill after bill on the car seat between us. It took a while. "One thousand four hundred and ninety, one thousand four hundred and ninety-five, one thousand five hundred, one thousand five hundred and five . . ." I paused and took a deep breath before I laid down the final bill. "One thousand five hundred and ten dollars. Holy. Cow." We sat staring at the money, stunned.

One thousand five hundred and ten dollars. Not a million, but more money than we'd ever seen before, and I began to say as much to Ralph when I was interrupted by a loud crash from behind the car. We both jumped and the money scattered.

Then the barn went quiet.

I crouched down in the seat. Muggers! I could picture tomorrow's headline: BELOVED KIDS FOUND MURDERED IN LOCAL BARN. I was happy to wait for my untimely death to find me, but Ralph signaled for us to check out the source of the crash. I shook my head. His eyed bulged and he mouthed "Come on!" Then he made a series of hand gestures, motioning for me to climb out my side before pointing to the back of the car. Since it was his idea, I let him go first.

I clambered out from my side of the car, my heart slamming in my chest, and began to creep toward the rear fender. At the moment I passed the trunk, I jumped and yelled "Gotcha!" as loud as I could, hoping to scare whoever or whatever it was away. The whoever or whatever it was screamed.

Pig Face. I should have known.

Lester was flat against the back of the car, clutching his heart, looking both embarrassed and terrified.

"What are you doing here?" Ralph and I said at the same time.

Lester being Lester, it didn't take him long to get

over being petrified and return to being his normal, annoying Pig Face self. "Isn't it obvious? I followed you here."

"Why?" I snapped. I don't know why I asked the question. I already knew the answer.

"I dunno. I wanted to see what you were up to."

"How long have you been following us?" Ralph demanded.

"Since you left Charlie at the house" was my rat brother's sullen reply. Lester's head hung low, showing off the massive cowlick that made his hair go crazily in three directions.

Since we'd left Charlie at the house? That meant he'd been following us for almost the entire afternoon! The only thing he'd missed was our run-in with Hazel and Zach.

"You're such a little sneak!" I leaned forward to give him a good shake but Ralph stopped me, holding up a hand and looking remarkably like a traffic cop.

"I'm sorry," Lester said, finally peering up at me. "I was just bored and you guys *did* blow me off. Oh, and you dropped some money," he added as an afterthought, pointing to the hundred-dollar bill on the floor beside me.

Ralph and I whipped around and began to frantically scoop up bills. Lester, no doubt thinking that helping us would put him back in our good graces, crawled under the car to grab one that had fallen beneath the engine.

He held it out to me. "Fifteen hundred and ten dollars is a lot of money."

I took the bill and sighed. "You heard everything."

He shook his head. "Not everything."

"What did you miss?" Ralph said, looking skeptical.

"What you said after holy cow," Lester replied.

I exploded. "We didn't say anything after that!" I went to grab for him again, forcing Ralph to stand between us once more.

"Let me at him!" I said, trying to reach around Ralph, which wasn't easy, given his size.

"Tracy, there's nothing we can do about it now," Ralph said. "It makes me wanna kill him, too, but what's done is done. It's not like he can un-know stuff."

I resented how reasonable Ralph was being. He

should be riled up, too. Lester had no business snooping on us! Who knew what he would do with his new-found knowledge?

Meanwhile, Pig Face had turned full-on detective. "Who do you think the money belongs to? I saw Joe Tunney on the track—do you think it's his? Maybe it belongs to one of the baseball teams. It's too bad we were out of town. I have no idea who played last night."

I shook my head, looked up at the barn ceiling, and counted to ten. "I'm not going to dignify your questions with a response. Go home and stop spying on us, or else I'll tell Mom!"

Lester smirked. I knew that smirk well. It was the one he used when he had something he could use against me.

"You can't make me go home. If you tell on me, I'll tell on you."

My excitement fizzled, leaving a sour taste in my mouth. He had me. If Pig Face told Mom that would be the end of my dream of fame and rewards. My only chance was to bargain with him, and from experience, I knew that was almost always impossible.

I held up my hands. "What do you want?"

Lester knew he had me over a barrel. He thrust out his chest and crossed his arms. "I want to help you guys find out whose money it is."

"No way—" Ralph began, but I held my hand up and shushed him.

"You'll have to listen to us," I said, looking into those Pig Face eyes. "And you can't say anything to Mom or Dad about this unless we say you can."

"Fine. And *you* can't say anything to them about me following you," he countered. "*And* you have to listen to my ideas."

The thought of listening to Pig Face made my toes curl. On the other hand, the idea of stuffing him into the trunk of the car was very appealing. Still, what choice did I have? Pig Face had won. Now my only hope was to somehow keep him under control.

I nodded. "Fine."

We gave each other a solemn nod and then spat in our hands and shook on it.

Ralph shook his head. "You two are gross. Okay— so we're stuck with Lester. Now we have to figure out what's next." He began to count the money to make sure we'd picked it all up.

"I think we should hide the money and check around. See if we can figure out who lost it," I said.

Ralph nodded, but Pig Face began to hop up and down like a windup rabbit. "What do you mean *we'll hide the money?* Shouldn't we call the police or put the money back or put an ad in the paper?"

I bit my lip. I wasn't going to tell Pig Face that if we did any of the things he'd suggested we wouldn't be heroes. We had to find the money's owner ourselves and return it with all the pomp and ceremony such an act required. Suddenly an image of Zach reading the *St. Croix Courier*, admiring my picture on the front page as he marveled at how exciting St. Stephen was, popped into my head. No, I was *definitely* solving this myself.

I looked at Lester scornfully. "It's a mystery, Pig Face!"

"We—meaning, Ralph and me, and now, unfortunately, you—are going to figure this out on our own. We don't need grown-ups. We can solve this ourselves. It'll be exciting!"

"Plus, if we turn the money in, maybe the police will charge *us* with stealing," Ralph added. I could tell from the look on Ralph's face that he was worried this might be true but was trying hard not to show it.

Lester looked nervous. I waited for the hives. Maybe he'd decide it was too much for him and he'd abandon the idea of working with us. "I'm not sure . . ."

I gave him my hardest stare and said the one thing that I knew would get him on board: "Don't you want to help Ralph and me? Be part of the team?"

Lester's eyes were as big and round as the old head-lights on the Model T. This was an offer he couldn't refuse. "I'm in," he said, reaching into his pocket for a tissue and blowing his nose. *Dust,* he mouthed to me. Then he added, "But no more calling me Pig Face, okay?"

I nodded. I'd started calling Lester *Pig Face* when he was four and used to chase me around the house, snorting like a little pig. The name had stuck, although I usually reserved it for when he was really annoying or when I wanted to make him mad. It wasn't going to be easy to stop calling him names, but if it meant he wouldn't tell Mom, it would probably be worth it.

"I'll try," I said. "But you have to try not to be a Pig Face."

Lester nodded begrudgingly.

I smiled at Ralph. "Hey, we have our summer project!"

"Woohoo!" Ralph stretched his arm out in front of him and gestured for Lester and me to do the same. We locked hands and then Ralph said, "One, two, three— Team Huffman-Munroe!"

Lester's eyes shined. "This is just like being on a hockey team," said the most un-athletic boy in St. Stephen.

Ralph laughed. "Only it's better, because you don't have to keep falling on your butt on the ice or worry that someone's going to bump into you," said the second most un-athletic boy in St. Stephen.

I nodded, but more out of sympathy than agreement. And I definitely didn't like that there were now two Munroes on Team Huffman-Munroe.

"The first thing we need to do is figure out where to hide the money," I said.

"We could hide it here, in the barn," Ralph suggested.

I looked around. The Attwoods had stuff everywhere. Tools hung from hooks in the wall; the lawn mower was parked beside the Weedwacker near a pile of old tires. "Too risky. Mr. and Mrs. A. are in here all the time. It should be somewhere no one will stumble upon it, and that only we know about."

"Like where?" Lester asked.

Ralph and I seemed to have the exact same thought at the exact same time. "The Big Rock!"

"What's the Big Rock?" Lester asked.

I smiled. "You're about to find out, Pig Face. I mean, um, Lester. We're about to show you our secret lair."

CHAPTER 5

Before heading off to the Big Rock, we stopped at home so Lester could go to the bathroom. His bladder was going to be a problem. On top of the hay fever and allergies that made him a human sneeze factory, you could set your watch by Lester having to go to the bathroom every hour on the hour. Mom said the constant bathroom breaks were related to his nerves. All I knew was we'd have to include plenty of pit stops in our plans.

While Ralph and I waited for Lester, I stared out the large living room picture window that faced in the direction of the dugout. Of course, I couldn't see the dugout because of the trees, but I could imagine it. In my mind, it had become a place of excitement and secrets. Probably once we returned the money to its rightful owner the town would want to erect a plaque at the baseball field in Ralph's and my honor. Something like: THIS DUGOUT IS WHERE TRACY MUNROE AND RALPH HUFFMAN FOUND MONEY AND BECAME HEROES. As I stood there daydreaming, I saw something out of the corner of my eye. Zach was cutting through the trees behind my house, heading to the baseball field. I couldn't help but admire how mature and confident he looked as he loped along.

"Whatcha looking at?"

I jumped at Ralph's question. I'd forgotten he was in the room, too. When I pointed at Zach, Ralph snorted. "He's everywhere. I hope he gets poison ivy."

I laughed. "There's no poison ivy in those woods."

"Maybe we should plant some."

"I can't believe how much you're letting this guy bug you. Normally nothing bothers you, except maybe a cake that doesn't rise."

Ralph sighed. "I know. I feel about him how you feel about Jasmine."

"We definitely need to avoid him then."

"All set!" Lester was back, dragging a knapsack behind him, *bump, bump, bump.*

Ralph watched with amusement as Lester tried, unsuccessfully, to hoist the beast onto his scrawny shoulders. When it fell to the ground for the third time with Lester still attached, Ralph leaned over and tapped my brother on the shoulder. "What's with the knapsack? We'll be gone for an hour, tops."

"Supplies," Lester said decisively. "If we're going to solve a mystery, we need supplies." He managed to right himself and started for the door, only to fall over again. He reminded me of the little dog, Max, in *How the Grinch Stole Christmas*.

Ralph gave me a *what on Earth?* look, grabbed the knapsack, and slung it across his own shoulders. Lester got back up, a big grin spreading across his face like a rising sun in a universe of freckles.

"What kind of supplies?" I asked.

"You'll see." Lester loves to be mysterious and it's so annoying.

Our first destination wasn't far: the train tracks

that ran perpendicular to Marks Street. I stopped and looked both ways. The train only passes by three times a day—at eight o'clock, five o'clock, and around seven-thirty—but I liked to be sure, all the same. As I turned left to follow the guys, satisfied that I'd live another day, I caught a glimpse of something red slipping into the bushes farther down the tracks to my right. Curious, I waited to see if I could catch sight of whatever it was again, but after several seconds of seeing nothing, I ran to catch up with Ralph and Lester.

We exited where the tracks passed the Junkyard, which isn't a junkyard at all, just part of a gravel pit where people dump old machinery and other garbage. The rust and weeds that have taken over the equipment make the place feel wild and dangerous, and I'd often seen teenagers hanging out there on hot summer evenings. Despite the ruin, it had always been a place of lost treasures: an owl brooch I'd discovered beside an old tractor, the Red Sox cap Ralph found hanging from a nearby tree. You had to brave the Junkyard if you wanted to get to the Big Rock.

Ralph and I'd discovered the Big Rock the previous

summer during one of our many expeditions. It's exactly what it sounds like: a massive boulder ten feet high and thirty feet long located in the forest that borders the gravel pit. It isn't easy to reach, which ups its secret lair potential. To get there, we had to cross Dennis Stream, hopping from one slimy stone to the next, walk straight for a quarter of a mile, scramble over some other smaller boulders, and then make the final ascent to the top. We'd tried to think of a more interesting name than the Big Rock, but nothing had stuck. It had been our place to talk or to hide from annoying brothers. But now that we were showing Lester where it was, Ralph and I had lost our secret hangout. That made me kind of sad.

The forest was peaceful—just the odd chirp of a bird and the buzz of insects, interrupted now and then by the *boom-boom* sound of a dump truck loading gravel back at the pit. Shafts of dappled light touched the path here and there, little beacons guiding us onward. I taught Lester how to avoid tripping over tree roots and how to use the crevices on the side of the Big Rock as handholds. He scrambled up behind me without any trouble, and I could tell that he was impressed with himself.

At the top, I surveyed our rocky kingdom. "This is where we hold our meetings," I said, plopping down on a green carpet of moss, still slightly damp from the dew that never quite dried this far into the forest.

Lester looked around, thrilled.

Meanwhile, Ralph reached up, grabbed a thermal bag we'd left hanging on a nearby branch, and plunked down. He unzipped the top, pulled out a package of Ganong pink peppermints—also made at the local chocolate factory and our meeting candy of choice—and popped one into his mouth before passing the bag to me.

I took one and handed Lester the package. "So what do you think of our secret lair?"

"I didn't know this place existed. I've never been in these woods. It's awesome."

I nodded, satisfied. It *was* awesome.

Settling himself on a particularly cushy spot, Lester reached over and took back his knapsack from Ralph. He unzipped it and pulled out three bottles of water, his asthma inhaler, a box of candy corn he'd bought in Old Orchard Beach, a set of cheap walkie-talkies he got last Christmas, and an iPad.

"You took Dad's iPad!" I said in horror, reaching out to rescue it. "He's gonna kill you!"

Pig Face was too quick and managed to evade my grasp. "He's napping. Mom says he's tired after the long drive and two weeks at the beach. She said I could borrow it to play games."

"Yeah, but she didn't mean you could take it out of the house!" I protested. I watched as he powered it up and typed in Dad's password.

"She didn't say I couldn't. Besides, we need it to do research. First, we should see if anyone's reported any missing money."

"He's got a point." Ralph crunched his peppermint to smithereens and reached for a piece of candy corn. "I wish I had a tablet. Does your dad like this one?"

Lester loved to talk about boring stuff like computers and Ralph had just opened up a whole can of boring stuff for Lester to chew on.

"He does. It's interesting, because—"

"Focus, Lester," I interrupted. "You're right. We need to do some research. Start with the local paper and then try the big-city ones. See if anyone's reported lost or stolen money."

Ralph and I leaned in close on either side of my brother to see the screen. A couple of taps later and we were at the home page of the *St. Croix Courier*. After searching several days' worth of news, it was clear that if someone lost money, they hadn't reported it to the paper. We checked the big papers—the *Telegraph Journal* and the *Daily Gleaner*—but found nothing there, either.

"What about Facebook?" Ralph asked. "Maybe someone's talking about it there."

I started to say that neither Lester nor I had an account because we were too young when suddenly Dad's Facebook page popped up, a big picture of him with his arms around Lester and me filling the screen.

"Pig Face—I mean Lester—how'd you do that?"

"I just watched Dad log in and memorized his password," Lester said, as if it was the most natural thing in the world. *Why didn't I think of that?* I thought about how much trouble Lester would get in when I told Dad about his account being hacked, then realized sadly that my days of ratting Lester out were over now that we were working together on this mystery.

Dad owned a sporting goods store, which meant he pretty much knew everyone in town. Or so it seemed to me: he had over seventeen hundred friends and the population of St. Stephen is only around five thousand. I thought there was a pretty good chance if anyone had lost a bunch of money, *someone* would be talking about it on Facebook.

"I can't believe how many grown-ups are playing games online," I snorted, as we saw yet another person crowing about getting a high score on Milltown Monster Mash.

"Yeah, and look at how many of them are talking about the weather," Lester added. "'Jack Fletcher wishes it would cool down,' 'Tammy Doyle hopes it rains soon.' Who cares about the weather?"

He continued to scroll down the screen, past barbecue pictures, birthday celebrations, funny cat videos, and inspirational messages. After hundreds of posts, it was clear that no one was talking about the money we'd found.

"Here's something interesting," Lester said, more to himself than to Ralph and me.

"What is it?" I shoved in closer to get a better look.

Hazel McNutt's face was beaming at me. *Yuck.* I wanted to keep scrolling to get away from her, except Lester was right: it *was* interesting. She wasn't alone in the picture. There was an old guy with silvery-white hair sitting beside her, his arm outstretched, obviously taking the selfie. I checked the date. Hazel had posted the picture last night.

I read the caption out loud. "Me and John Favola—a.k.a. The Silver Fox, LOL—cuddling after our walk." Hazel's post had fifteen likes. Even my dad had liked it for crying out loud.

I looked over at Ralph. "Yuck."

Ralph leaned away from the screen. "If Mr. Favola is anything like Zach, double-yuck. Hazel's going to regret dating him."

Given how mean Hazel had been to me earlier, I wasn't really interested in her regrets. I was thinking of poor Zach and how awful it must be for him that his father was dating Hazel.

It was Lester who brought us back to the task at hand: "Earth to Tracy and Ralph. Who cares if Hazel McNutt and Mr. Favola are dating? We still don't know who left the paper bag at the dugout."

I didn't want to admit it, but he had a point. Whose money was this, anyway?

Chapter 6

The three of us sat staring at the bag of money like it was some kind of sculpture in an art gallery. I could imagine one of those little white cards in front of it with some snooty title typed on it like Paper Bag Mystery.

After a few minutes of silence, Lester began to squirm. "If we can't figure out whose money it is, do we get to keep it? 'Cause if we can, I think we should use the money to buy candy and games, maybe take a trip."

Lester had changed back into Pig Face.

"We will solve the mystery of whose money this is. We're going to be heroes, not thieves." I looked across at Ralph and could tell we were both thinking the same thing: *Why'd we have to get saddled with Pig Face?*

"I said '*if* we can't figure out whose money it is,' so stop getting all wound up," Lester protested. "Okay, we've looked at the newspapers and Facebook. How else can we figure out who it belongs to?"

Good question.

I leaned over and nabbed another peppermint. "I'm sure this money is stolen."

Ralph gave me a confused look. "Elaborate," he said.

I stuck out my tongue before continuing. "Well duh, isn't it obvious?"

He shook his head. "Not to me it isn't. We can't see inside your brain, Tracy. Elaborate."

The amount Ralph loved to say that word was equal to how much I hated to hear it. "Fine, Mr. I-want-to-know-every-boring-detail; I will elaborate! Think about it: Someone leaves a paper bag full of money in a baseball dugout? Does that make any sense? If you or I'd lost that much money, we'd be searching everywhere for it. We'd be freaking out! Who takes over fifteen hundred dollars to a baseball field, anyway? And the paper bag was all mixed up with dirt and leaves. That makes me think someone was trying to *hide* it."

"I don't know, Tracy," Lester said. I could feel my face starting to flush. *He didn't know?*

"Elaborate," Ralph told Lester. I crunched my peppermint harder.

Lester stood up and began to pace around the top of the rock, his fingers laced behind his back as if he were a lawyer in a courtroom. He loved being the center of attention and it was clear he'd been watching too many courtroom shows on TV with Dad. I was surprised he hadn't said "I object!" when I'd said I thought the money was stolen.

"First of all, how do we know someone *isn't* looking for the money? Maybe they didn't call the papers or put it on Facebook because they're afraid the whole town would be out looking for it. Or maybe they don't want anyone to know they've lost the money."

"He's got a point," Ralph said. "Some people would go searching just to keep it for themselves. Not everyone's as nice as we are. And maybe whoever lost it doesn't want people to know that they carry that much money around."

"Or maybe they don't know where they lost the

money," Lester continued. "Maybe they're searching all over town for it."

I hated that some of his ideas were good.

"You have some good points, Pig F—I mean Lester—but I think the fact that it was wedged under the bench means it was probably hidden by someone, and the only reason you'd hide a paper bag full of money is if you'd stolen it."

"She has a point," Ralph said.

Lester snorted. "You guys think everything is a mystery. Don't you remember what happened in fourth grade, Tracy?"

I winced. "This isn't like that."

Lester raised his eyebrows so high they nearly touched his hairline. "Are you sure? Remember the award they gave you?"

I gave him the stink eye. I'd been trying to forget that award for over a year.

"*Girl Most Likely to Find the Loch Ness Monster*," Ralph added, unhelpfully.

In fourth grade, Ralph and I decided we were going to be famous detectives when we grew up, just like

Humphrey Bogart in *The Maltese Falcon*. I couldn't talk Ralph into wearing a trench coat, but we did borrow my mom's magnifying glass so we could look for clues. We'd wander the playground, me clutching my top-secret detective notebook, interviewing kids and teachers trying to find and solve mysteries. Unfortunately, St. Stephen Elementary School was totally without crimes. It was very discouraging.

At first, our homeroom teacher, Mrs. Garnett, thought it was funny that my detective notebook had a page about each of the school's teachers and Principal Walton. But after I showed her the page where I suspected Principal Walton's new Cadillac was stolen because she'd gone out of town to pick it up, Mrs. Garnett suggested I keep my suspicions to myself and my detective notebook at home. Of course, I couldn't do that—a detective's notebook is everything to her—but I made sure to keep it hidden, which meant I was forced to write up all of my notes while sitting on a toilet in the girls' bathroom. Still, I guess I wasn't as good at keeping it hidden as I thought, because at the end-of-year assembly, Principal Walton gave me that stupid award. Jasmine has never let me live it down. And now, here was Pig Face throwing it in my face at the exact moment Ralph and I had *finally* found a case.

"This isn't like fourth grade, Lester. This is a real mystery! That's a bag full of money," I said, pointing to the crumpled paper sack in front of us. "Maybe the person stuck it under the bench because they were being chased. They planned to come back for it as soon as the coast was clear. That's what I'd do. I'd hide the stash someplace where people wouldn't be looking for money."

Lester knew better than to argue. "Okay, if that's what happened, it would mean the bag hasn't been there very long and that you and Ralph took it before they could come back for it. Did you see anyone else besides Joe Tunney hanging around? I was too busy eavesdropping on you two to notice anything unusual." He grinned his best jack-o'-lantern grin, the one I always wanted to wipe off his face.

"Jasmine Singh and her friends were leaving when we arrived," I said.

Ralph looked troubled. "Joe didn't even look at us. I doubt he had anything to do with the bag of money."

"I hope no one besides me saw you guys find the bag," Lester said, suddenly looking nervous. A blotchy hive was forming on his left cheek.

I thought of the flash of red I'd seen earlier. "When we were walking over here, I thought I saw someone near the train tracks. What if someone *did* see us take the money? What if they followed us here?" The BELOVED KIDS FOUND MURDERED IN LOCAL BARN headline was replaced by a new one: BELOVED KIDS FOUND MURDERED ON BIG ROCK. I shivered.

Ralph and Lester stopped chomping their peppermints. Without saying a word, Ralph and I hopped up and quietly patrolled the top of the Big Rock, checking the woods below while Lester frantically repacked his knapsack. No one was there. Ralph and I sat down again, but we were jumpy and kept standing up, in case we had to leave in a hurry.

After doing this three or four times, I'd had enough. "We need to leave. We're like sitting ducks up here." Everything about the woods felt scary all of a sudden. Even the birds' songs sounded sinister to me.

"Before we go, we have to hide the money," Lester reminded us.

"You're right. Any ideas where?" Ralph picked up the paper bag and looked around.

"Let's hide it down near the base of the Big Rock and then go home. I'm starving," I said, even though I was thinking *I'm scared*. "We'll work on this again tomorrow morning. How about you come over to our place at nine o'clock sharp, Ralph?"

"Can we make it nine-thirty? I watch a baking show every morning at nine o'clock. Tomorrow's episode is about fondant." I wanted to say something nasty to Ralph about having to adjust our detecting schedule around the Food Network, but I thought better of it and nodded.

We climbed back down and tucked the bag into a crevice hidden by brambly shrubs. It was as good a spot as any and was protected if it rained.

"Looks like we're on the case," Lester said, beaming up at Ralph and me.

Ralph smiled and gave Lester a high five. *That's going*

to go to his head, I thought. Sure enough, Lester turned, waiting for me to give him a high five, too. There was no way I was going to do that. But then Ralph gave me this look that said *don't be mean*. I sighed and half-heartedly slapped my hand against Lester's. He whooped with delight.

What Ralph didn't seem to get, but I knew too well, was that Pig Face was like glue. In the beginning it seems like he's just a harmless glue stick, something you can wash off easily with soap and water. Then he turns out to be crazy glue—you're stuck with him forever.

"Am I ever glad you're home, Tracy," Ralph said as we made our way back through the woods, keeping an eye out for any unwanted company. "It was so boring without you!"

CHAPTER 7

A few minutes later, Lester and I were approaching our house when I stopped, surprised. Zach was sitting on our front steps, looking at his cell phone.

"Who's that?" Lester asked.

"The kid who's living next door this summer," I said. "His name is Zach."

"He doesn't look like he belongs in St. Stephen," Lester mused. "He looks kind of . . ." He struggled to find the right word then added, "Sparkly!"

I giggled. It was a pretty good description. Especially since, as we approached him, I could see a gold chain with a pendant hanging around his neck, glittering in the sunlight. I didn't know any boys who wore jewelry.

As we walked toward him, all I could think about was how Ralph was not going to like Zach showing up at my place. And even though I knew I wouldn't be friends with Zach—I was Team Ralph, after all—I couldn't help but be a little excited that a good-looking boy from New York City was waiting for me.

When Zach saw us, he stood up. "Hey."

"Hey," I replied. His greeting sounded silky, while mine was more like a strangled chicken.

"You must be Lester," Zach said, extending a hand to my brother. "I'm Zach. I'm staying next door for the summer." I'd never seen a kid shake hands with another kid before. It was odd and impressive at the same time.

Lester took Zach's hand and gave it a vigorous shake. "Lester T. Munroe." I cringed.

"What's the T stand for?"

"Trouble," I supplied, but Lester was having none of it.

"Tiberius," he said. Lester loves his middle name, but I find it embarrassing that my dad gave him the same middle name as Captain Kirk from *Star Trek*. I waited for Zach's response with dread.

"*Tiberius* as in James *Tiberius* Kirk?" he asked.

Lester gave him a happy nod.

"Cool, man. My middle name is boring compared to that—Antonio, after my grandfather."

I thought Antonio was a pretty name; it sounded like music the way Zach pronounced it. Meanwhile, Lester's chest was still visibly puffed out from the compliment. Zach was creating a monster.

"You've got red hair, just like your sister."

"She takes after me," Lester joked.

Zach looked confused. "But I thought you were younger?"

"I am younger," Lester said. "But secretly, I'm as old as dirt." He gave his best Lester cackle. I was mortified. Zach stared at Lester as if he were trying to decide what to make of this kid—was he funny or weird? My money was on weird.

Zach thought differently. "You're a funny guy," he said.

In my head I shouted, *Stop! He will be insufferable to live with if you keep giving him compliments!* By the time Lester shared this story with Mom and Dad at supper it would have changed into Zach begging Lester to be his best friend. Lester's stories always involved people begging him to be their best friend, which wasn't that surprising, I guess, considering Lester didn't have a lot of friends.

"A funny guy who's going inside," I replied. Lester grinned and began skipping toward the door. He was putting on quite a show.

Zach watched his retreating back. "Your brother's a real character, huh?"

"You don't know the half of it," I said. I was still shocked to see Zach again so soon. When he'd said he wanted to hang out, I wasn't expecting it to actually happen, especially after Ralph had told me that Zach and Jasmine were inseparable.

"I know you just got back, but do you have time for a walk? I've been waiting for you to come home for over an hour. Your mom had no idea where you were." I pulled the phone out of my pocket. There were six missed calls from Mom. I was going to have some serious explaining to do.

"I can tell you where we were," a squeaky voice

behind us said. I'd thought Lester had gone into the house, but I was wrong. The door was slightly ajar, allowing him to eavesdrop on me. Again. I was about to yell for Mom when I remembered the handshake promise in the barn. Not being able to rat on Lester was already getting to be a problem. Instead, I glared at him and shook my head slightly, which seemed to work. He clamped his mouth shut. No way was any-one finding out the location of our secret woodland retreat.

"I'm not sure I have time for a walk," I said, pre-tending to look down at my watch, which hadn't told the correct time for months because I kept forgetting to ask Dad to help me change the battery. I might be interested in hearing about New York City, but I wasn't interested in arguing about it with Ralph later.

"Come on—you must have ten minutes. We can go sit there and talk," Zach said, pointing to a bench that was near the end of Hazel's driveway under a gnarly old apple tree that always kind of reminded me of Hazel herself.

I waffled. Talking to Zach for ten minutes was

hardly "hanging out," so Ralph couldn't be mad about that, right?

"I guess so," I said, and was rewarded with the movie star smile again. I poked my head in through the door, practically knocking into Lester, who was pretending to straighten the shoes in the bottom of the hall closet. "Tell Mom I'm going to hang with Zach for about ten minutes, okay?"

"Okay, but don't do anything I wouldn't do!" Lester said, much too loudly. I counted to ten and prayed the earth would swallow me, then turned and followed Zach.

Either Zach hadn't heard Pig Face or he was too polite to say anything. "That Les seems like a good kid," Zach said. Even if I was mad at my brother, I was glad Zach liked him. It meant he had a good sense of humor. I thought about telling him that Lester detested being called Les as much as he disliked being called Pig Face, but then thought better of it.

We reached the apple tree and I plopped down on the bench. The street was empty, which was unfortunate, because I knew everyone at school would be impressed if they saw me hanging out with an older kid from New York City. Well, everyone but Ralph. I kind of wished Jasmine would show up again. She'd go nuts if she saw Zach and me sitting together. Just the thought of that made me smile.

"You seem like you're in a good mood," Zach said. I was glad he couldn't read my thoughts. "So where were you guys?"

"Hanging out," I said, trying to sound cool and mysterious.

"Just you and Les?"

"No, Ralph was there, too. We were just walking around the neighborhood."

"I don't think Ralph likes me very much," Zach said, running his hands through his floppy hair. I wasn't sure how to respond. Telling Zach Ralph didn't like him seemed rude, but I couldn't tell him he was wrong. In the end, I said nothing. "I was so bored this afternoon," Zach continued. "Maybe I could have hung out with you guys if Ralph liked me more. Every time he comes over to Hazel's, he pretty much ignores me."

I was confused. Ralph had only mentioned one visit

to Hazel's. But Zach made it sound like Ralph had been there a lot. What was up?

"Never mind," he said. "I don't want to put you on the spot about Ralph."

I wasn't sure how to respond to that either, so I continued to say nothing, which was not like me at all. In fact, I was feeling downright uncomfortable and wished I'd never agreed to sit with Zach.

I glanced down. The two of us couldn't have been dressed more differently. I was in the vintage shorts and peasant blouse I'd snagged at Trixie's, lime-green loafers on my feet. Zach's jeans and T-shirt were trendy, like he'd stepped out of a Summer Style spread in *Seventeen*. I could tell everything he was wearing was expensive, while my outfit probably cost twenty bucks.

"Do you like it here?" I finally asked.

Zach leaned back on the bench and crossed his arms behind his head. "I don't know. I miss my mom. There are so many things going on in New York City in the summer. It's hard to find anything to do here. My dad's lined up some work for me—mowing lawns, doing odd jobs—because he doesn't want me to get bored or get into trouble. I start after supper. But I've never mowed a lawn in my life. My mom and I live in an apartment building and there's no grass. Plus, last week I needed a new bathing suit and I couldn't find one here. There's like, what, five stores in this whole town? And don't get me started on the restaurants. Dad and I still haven't found a decent place to eat yet."

"We have the Lobster Hut," I offered. "They make a good lobster roll."

"And you know what else? I can't even get my favorite candy bars here!"

"Do you mean chocolate bars? Mr. Brown has lots of different kinds at his store."

Zach pulled a half-eaten bar, with its wrapper still on, out of his pocket. "They don't have this," he said dismissively.

I reached over and took a look at the black label. "Dylan's Candy Bar, Belgian Dark Chocolate," I read aloud. "I've never heard of that. Have you had any of the chocolate from Ganong's yet?"

"No. But I bet it's not as good as this. This is, like, only the best candy bar ever."

"I don't think you can say that until you try Ganong's chocolate," I said, anxious to defend the honor of what I considered to be the best chocolate in the world.

Zach laughed. "Okay, I'll try it. Meanwhile—have a bite of this." He broke off a piece and passed it over. I popped it in my mouth and smiled. It *was* good. But I didn't think it was better than Ganong's. Close, but not better.

"If we don't sell them around here, how'd you get this one?"

"My mom took pity on me and mailed me a box. I just got it today. If she hadn't sent me some, I don't think I could last the summer here."

"Your mom sounds nice."

Zach looked down at the chocolate bar in his hand and smiled. "Yeah, she is. I miss her. She and I do lots of fun things together. Every summer we go to Coney Island and the Bronx Zoo. I won't get to do either of those things this summer."

A small sigh escaped me as I thought about all the wonderful things a person could do in New York City.

"I get why you miss home. I've always wanted to go to New York City."

Zach smiled. "You should go! It's great!"

"Do you ever go see plays on Broadway?"

I got a snort in response. "Do I? Like every single month. My mom loves musicals and we go all the time."

"Do you like them?" I loved musicals. I wanted to ask him all kinds of questions about what he'd seen, but I was afraid he wouldn't think they were cool.

"In the beginning, I kind of thought they were a snore, but then I saw how much my mom loved them, so now I guess I like them, too."

I suddenly became regular Tracy again. "I love them! I listen to all kinds of Broadway music. Someday, I'm going to see a real, live musical on Broadway. My mom says she'll take me when I'm sixteen. A couple of years ago, a touring production of *Cats* went to Saint John, which is only an hour from here. My mom and dad took me. I loved it so much I cried."

I wasn't sure if telling a strange boy that I'd cried during *Cats* was a good idea, but Zach's response laid my fears to rest. "I love *Cats*! My mom plays that album all the time. We even have a cat named after one of the characters—Rum Tum Tugger!"

"That is the best cat name ever! Have you see *Wicked? Phantom of the Opera? Hamilton?*"

"Yes, yes, and no."

"Les Miserables?"

Zach laughed and began to hum a song from the show. I joined in, and for the next couple of minutes we were doing a pretty fair rendition of "One Day More" when we were interrupted by the creak of Hazel's front door. *That woman is a witch,* I thought. *She always knows when I'm near her house. And she always knows how to spoil a good time.*

"Zach, are you out there?" Hazel called. I scrunched down a bit. Zach and I were hidden by the tree trunk. I didn't think she could see me and I was glad. Maybe I could avoid having two conversations with Hazel in one day.

"I'm here," he called, smirking at me. "How can I help you, Miss Hazel?"

Calling her Miss Hazel made the witch giggle. "Zach Favola, you're a scamp!"

Zach raised an eyebrow. "Only with you, Hazel," he called back.

Another giggle. "Silly boy. Your father just called. He wants you to go to his office right away." There were no giggles attached to what she said next. "Is Tracy Munroe with you? Her mother's looking for her."

"Yes, she's here."

"Then send her home right now."

"Maybe you can fly me home on your broomstick," I muttered as I stood up.

Zach gave me a look of surprise that morphed into delight. "You're funny!" he said.

I grinned. "Maybe just a little bit. Hazel and I have a history of not getting along."

We stepped out from under the tree. Zach went right, in the direction of downtown. I went left to go home, forced to walk past Hazel's evil eye.

I was almost past her when she said my name, like a command or some evil spell. "Tracy Munroe!" she repeated. I turned and looked at her, waiting for the lecture.

"You leave that boy alone." She wagged a bejeweled

finger at me. "He's a good boy with a wonderful father and he doesn't have time for your silliness."

Silliness? Anger washed over me like a tsunami. How dare she tell me to leave him alone, like I was some ridiculous, mooning girl? He'd asked me to talk, not the other way around. She should save her comments for someone like Jasmine, who deserved them.

Then it hit me: Maybe Hazel was worried I'd tell Zach about how awful she and Jasmine were. Maybe she thought if I told Zach, he would tell his dad and they'd move out of her house to get away from her. *That would teach you a lesson, Hazel McNutt,* I thought.

As I turned to go, I couldn't help muttering under my breath, "The only person who's silly with men is you, Hazel."

I swear I hadn't meant for her to hear me. She *shouldn't* have been able to hear me. But somehow she did. There was a small gasp, as if I'd slapped her. Like a turtle retreating back into its shell, the big red hair was pulled back into the house and the front door slammed shut.

I stood there, stunned. I knew I should knock and

apologize. That would be the right thing to do. But my feelings were hurt, too, and Hazel had started it, not me. Still, I felt awful, which made me angry. I had more important things to think about than Hazel's dumb feelings. I needed to find out who the bag of money belonged to so I could be famous. And then Hazel would be sorry she was ever mean to me.

CHAPTER 8

I could hardly wait for Ralph to arrive the next morning. I was itching to begin solving the case. Standing in the open doorway, eyes and body facing left, toes tapping, I waited to catch the first glimpse of him. He made me almost jump out of my skin when he suddenly appeared on my right.

"You nearly scared me to death! Why'd you come the long way?" I demanded.

I got a shrug in return as Ralph passed over a Tupperware container filled with warm blueberry muffins. The smell of vanilla and blueberry was intoxicating and made me forget any questions I might have had. Why couldn't they make a perfume like *that*? When they did, I'd buy Hazel McNutt the first bottle to replace the hideous stuff she always wore. As soon as I thought of Hazel, I wished I hadn't; it made me feel bad again. But even if I wanted to apologize—which I wasn't sure I did—she probably wouldn't accept it anyway.

Lester squirmed his way into the space between us. "Ralph, I love you," he said, grabbing the fattest muffin. Charlie stood near the table waiting for the inevitable Lester crumb-fest.

"I'm not sure that was the reaction I was going for, Lester," Ralph said. Still, he looked pleased. Turning to me, he said, "What's on the agenda this morning?"

Before responding, I reached for the next biggest muffin before Lester could get his grubby paws back in the container. "I thought we should check around; you know, talk to people, see if anyone knows anything about missing money. I thought we could start at Trixie's. A lot of her customers tell her secrets, so she might have heard about the money. Then we should go to Brown's Store, since it's right here in the neighborhood. He might have seen something suspicious. If that doesn't help us, I say we stake out the ball field."

I swallowed a bite of muffin and understood Lester's reaction. "Hey, these are good. New recipe?"

Ralph nodded. "I've been testing the amount of sugar and vanilla I add. These are the best ones yet."

"Did you ask Zach if he'd seen anything suspicious when you were talking to him yesterday?" Lester asked me as he inspected the muffins to see which one was the blueberry-est.

Ralph stiffened. "You were talking to Zach again? When?"

"When we got home yesterday," I said. "And no, I didn't ask him if he'd seen anything suspicious. He doesn't even know anybody in town." I went to reach for another muffin, but Ralph pulled the container away from me. Surprised, I looked up at him. His eyes were narrowed, like he thought I was holding something back.

"What did he want?"

I squinted back at Ralph and put my hands on my hips. "He didn't want anything. He was just bored. I sat with him under Hazel's apple tree for about ten minutes and then I went home. End of story."

"What did he say?"

"You're acting like you're a police detective. He didn't *say* anything, not really. Apparently, his dad got him a job mowing lawns and doing yard work. And he said he misses New York City and his mom. Then I had to go home and he had to go meet his dad." I purposely did not mention our conversation about Broadway musicals, worried that Ralph might feel weird that Zach and I had something in common that Ralph and I didn't. I also didn't share my run-in with Hazel. It was too embarrassing.

Ralph put the container back on the table and sighed. "You know I don't like him."

"So don't like him," I said. "It's not like you have to be besties or anything. I bet I'll hardly see him this summer. You said it yourself—he likes Jasmine."

Ralph didn't look convinced.

"Zach said something about you being at Hazel's a lot?" I said, trying to change the subject.

"Zach should keep his mouth shut."

I waited to see if Ralph was going to explain. Instead, he grabbed a blueberry muffin and stuffed it in his mouth.

Ralph never kept secrets from me before. The idea that he might be now made me feel strange. At the same time, I didn't want to push it. Maybe there was a good reason he wasn't telling me. At least I hoped there was.

"Enough with the stupid Zach talk," Lester said, as if he hadn't been the one to bring him up to begin with. "Let's go to Trixie's!"

Mom poked her head around the corner. "Lester, we're leaving in ten minutes for the dentist."

"But, Mom!" Lester protested. "I'm busy!"

"No buts" was her firm reply. "You have to get that cavity filled. Go brush your teeth. Now."

Lester looked on the verge of tears. "Can you guys wait to go to Trixie's until I get back? I'll only be a couple hours."

I shook my head. "Lester, we have to start our investigation. You can help us as soon as you get back."

He nodded, his face an exact copy of those sad puppy pictures in the newspapers that make you want to go straight to the SPCA and bring home a new dog. Luckily for me, I was completely immune to his pathetic face. I'd seen it too many times.

"Hope the needle doesn't hurt too much, Brother Dear." I gave him my best sickeningly sweet smile, enjoying how big his eyes got when I said *needle*. My work done, I headed out the door with Ralph.

ℙ ℙ ℙ

When we walked into Trixie's, we were met by the jangling chorus of the long strings of bells that hung on the back of the door. The sound made me feel like I was arriving at a party, which wasn't too far from the truth. Trixie makes all of her customers feel like they're the guests of honor at a celebration she's thrown especially for them.

"Hallo-o!" came a muffled call from the back of the store. "I'll be right there!"

I leaned over the counter. Trixie was headfirst in an old trunk, digging through what appeared to be a nest of silk scarves and old belts. Items were pulled out and tossed behind her in a jumble. After a pink tutu flew up toward the massive crystal chandelier, I heard "Aha!"

Trixie stood up, her pink hair standing straight on end like some kind of cotton candy porcupine.

"Tracy! Ralph!" she cried in the overly dramatic voice she used for her favorite customers. "I haven't seen you for ages! How are you, my darlings?" Trixie is twenty-six years old, but sometimes she talks like my seventy-year-old Great Aunt Ruth.

"How's Trix?" Ralph said, heading toward an old china cabinet that contained antique shaving supplies and lighters. Ralph's positive he'll be shaving soon. I know he won't be.

"Ralph Huffman, I couldn't be better! It's summer, my boyfriend Jim *finally* got a job, and thanks to some amazing sleuthing on my part, I've just received the most divine shipment of old paint-by-number paintings." She turned her attention to me.

"Tracy Munroe, you are the most turned-out-woman in St. Stephen on this fine day. Tell me you watched some of the Audrey Hepburn film fest on TV last night?"

I grinned and nodded, looking down at the long fringed skirt I was wearing, a purchase from the store right before I went away on vacation. Trixie always puts things aside for me, always gives me a discount because she knows that my allowance is limited, and always is willing to listen to whatever Ralph and I have been up to.

"Have you gotten in anything new I'd like?" I asked.

Trixie's laugh was like the bells on the door. She reached under the counter and pulled out a shallow wicker basket. The stack of thin brass bracelets that were always on her right arm clanged together. Another "Aha!" and she triumphantly pulled out a small rhinestone brooch.

When she put it in my palm and I took a closer look, I could see it was a tiny, glittering book. "It's beautiful," I whispered.

Ralph had returned to my side and leaned over to see what it was.

"Wow," he said, "that must be worth a million bucks." I couldn't help but think of the paper bag of money hidden out at the Big Rock and what it could buy.

"How much is it?" I asked, dreading the response.

"For you, my sweet? Ten dollars."

I opened my mouth to protest—it was worth way more than that—but Trixie held up her hand.

"Ten dollars, and not another word or I'll reduce it to nine," she said. "I've been saving it for you. It came in while you were out of town. I knew you'd love it!"

Ralph nudged me and mouthed *money*. "Okay, she's taking it, Trixie," he said, "but we actually didn't come to shop."

"Ooo, sounds exciting!" Trixie said as she took the ten-dollar bill I'd pulled from my pocket—the last of my savings.

"We're actually doing some sleuthing this morning," I said.

"Cool." She wrote up the receipt and clipped the price tag off the back of the pin so I could put it on right away. "Are you Humphrey Bogart and Mary Astor or are you William Powell and Myrna Loy?"

Ralph looked at me, confused, and waited for me to

respond. He and I hadn't watched any William Powell and Myrna Loy movies together yet.

"Definitely Humphrey Bogart and Mary Astor," I said. William Powell and Myrna Loy played a married couple who were always solving cases in the *Thin Man* movies, and I did not want anyone to think I was married to Ralph. Nope, I was definitely the mysterious Mary Astor in *The Maltese Falcon*.

"Oh," Trixie said. "I think your sleuthing may end quite tragically then. How can I help?"

"Have you heard of anything mysterious happening around here lately?" I asked.

Our pink hostess smiled. "I wish! What kind of mysterious thing are you thinking of?"

"Like someone losing something?"

Trixie shook her head. "Sorry, mademoiselle, I have heard nothing, nada. But if I do, I promise to call you and Ralph *tout de suite*! To change the subject to a more mundane topic, be sure to come back in a couple of weeks, okay? I'm getting in some vintage sweaters and jackets before fall—perfect for a girl who's starting sixth grade and needs to make a dramatic entrance. *Very* Mary Astor."

"As if she needs any encouragement to come back," Ralph said over his shoulder as he dragged me toward the door. We stopped for a moment outside, letting our eyes adjust to the sun.

"You know what?" Ralph asked.

"What?"

"If we stop and shop everywhere we go, we'll never solve this case!"

"Let's see how *you* do at Brown's."

☙ ☙ ☙

Brown's Store was Ralph's favorite hangout. How could it not be? One side of the store is painted like a giant ice cream sandwich, and the first thing you see when you walk in the door is a big glass cabinet full of candy. It's wonderful.

"I think this is what heaven will be like," Ralph once said to me when we were sitting on the bench out front, slurping our milk shakes. "You know, all the good things you like to eat. No one hassling you." It was hard to argue with his thinking.

We walked into the store, which was empty except for Mr. Brown himself, who was filling up the pop machine. He gave us a big smile, closed the front of the machine, and dried his hands on the old apron he wore over his trousers.

"What's up this morning?" he asked. "Did you have a good vacation, Tracy? I know Ralph missed you."

I knew the last comment would make Ralph feel embarrassed, so I pretended I hadn't heard it.

"I had a good time, thanks for asking. How have things been around here?"

"Good, though I couldn't find my car keys for two days last week and practically tore the store apart looking for them!"

I saw my chance and took it. "I hate it when I lose things, too. Anybody else lose anything recently?"

Mr. Brown gave me one of his intense stares, the one he usually saves for when he wants to scare kids into not shoplifting. "I don't think so. Why—did you find something?"

I didn't want to lie, but I didn't want to tell him the truth either.

"You know us. We're always looking for stuff," I said. "So it's good to know if people have lost anything in case we come across it." It was *kind of* the truth.

Mr. Brown raised an eyebrow, but shook his head. "I haven't heard of anyone losing anything. Actually, it's been pretty quiet around here this week. So many people are away on vacation. I'm just glad you two came in to keep me company. The only bit of excitement in the neighborhood I know about is that fellow and his son who're renting from Hazel for the summer. The kid's been in a lot."

Ralph made a strange huffing sound. I didn't need him to tell me what he was thinking. It was clear he did not like Zach hanging around *his* favorite store. Which was totally nuts, but I completely understood it. I felt the same way whenever Jasmine visited Hazel.

"Thanks, Mr. Brown. Keep us in mind if you hear anything," I said.

Now that I was done interrogating Mr. Brown, I turned, expecting to see Ralph waiting to buy his usual handful of red licorice. Instead, he stood with his back to me, his fists clenched by his side. I was confused for a second and then realized that the front door was opening and that Zach was walking through it. And right behind him, in all of her belly-baring-pink-clothing glory, was Jasmine Singh.

CHAPTER 9

Zach was all smiles. I couldn't say the same about Jasmine. She looked like she'd swallowed a fly and wanted to spit it right back out. At me.

"Hey, what are you guys up to?" Zach said.

"Leaving," Ralph said forcefully.

"Too bad," Zach said. "I just ran into Jasmine out front and we came in to get a couple of Cokes. I thought maybe we could all hang out. I was going to suggest that when I saw you this morning, Ralph."

Zach had seen Ralph this morning? Where? On the street? At Hazel's again? Why hadn't Ralph mentioned that to me? Ralph's secret was starting to seriously bug me.

Jasmine batted her spidery eyelashes at him and

giggled. "I think they're going somewhere, Zach. Aren't you, Tracy?" she asked in a tone that made it clear to me that she thought I was an idiot, but that to some nice, unsuspecting person like Zach might sound friendly. I knew better.

"Yeah, we have plans," I said, never taking my eyes off Jasmine. "Maybe some other time."

Jasmine was the first to break our staring contest. She turned to Zach and in a mocking voice said, "Tracy and Ralph got kicked off Hazel's property yesterday. It was so funny. They didn't even notice the KEEP OFF THE GRASS sign! Can you believe it?"

Zach snickered. I scowled.

She continued on, as if anyone cared what she had to say, each word more annoying than the one before. "It did kind of remind me of when you and I were sitting out on the grass—before it got sprayed, 'cause we're not stupid—watching the stars that night I stayed over with Aunt Hazel. That was so much fun."

Jasmine's bragging about looking at the stars with Zach made me sick. Honestly, it was as if she'd been put on Earth just to torment me.

But two could play that game. The smile I flashed Jasmine was so sweet it was like Ralph's chocolate fudge. "That sounds like so much fun, Jasmine. It reminds me of how much fun Zach and I had hanging out yesterday." The flustered look on Jasmine's face was my reward. Zach grinned. I could tell he was enjoying watching Jasmine and me trying to one up each other and I didn't like this new side of him. I grabbed Ralph's arm, yanking him forward. "Well, we gotta go."

"Will I see you later, Tracy?" Zach asked.

Six simple words, but it was like he'd set the store on fire. Jasmine looked furious, so of course I couldn't resist giving her a triumphant smile. Ralph looked like he wanted to shove Zach into the pop cooler. Mr. Brown just stood watching, a bemused smile on his face, like he'd seen all this drama before.

"Maybe," I stammered. Meanwhile, Ralph was already halfway out the door. I ran to catch up to those long legs.

"Wait!"

He wheeled around. "What was that 'maybe'? Are

you going to be friends with that guy, Tracy? Can't you see right through him?"

"I hardly know him. Chill out. I just wanted to get under Jasmine's skin. Isn't it obvious how much she likes him?" Even though the last part was technically true, I felt a little guilty that I wasn't telling Ralph the whole truth. I actually kind of liked Zach. It had been fun talking with him yesterday, especially the singing part. What had he done to make Ralph so angry?

It was the lie Ralph wanted to hear. His shoulders relaxed and he smiled. "She must be seething inside."

"Furious." I giggled. "We haven't learned anything useful this morning. Do you think we should talk to anyone else before lunch? I thought we'd wait and do the stakeout once Pig Face is back from the dentist."

"We could stop in and talk to Mr. and Mrs. Attwood on the way to your place."

I doubted that the Attwoods would be any more helpful than Trixie or Mr. Brown, and I had a sneaking suspicion that Ralph had another motive for stopping there. I pressed their doorbell three times—two short bursts and then one long one, my secret ring so Mrs. A. would know it was me. When she opened the door, we were greeted by the scent of freshly baked gingerbread. Not even Ralph could make gingerbread as tasty as Mrs. A.'s, which is exactly why he'd decided to add the Attwoods to our list of people to speak with.

"Perfect timing," she said, ushering us into the living room, where Mr. A. was sitting on the edge of his chair watching a baseball game. He was wearing his New York Yankees cap backward, which made him look kind of like a kid, except that he was old and balding. We took a seat on a nearby couch and I reached for some of the game snacks, only to have my knuckles rapped by Mr. A. as I grabbed a pretzel.

"Burns!" Mrs. A.'s tone warned her husband not to tease us. He sighed and passed over the bowl. On the screen I could see that the Yankees were down three-nothing to the Baltimore Orioles, which probably explained his grouchiness.

"Isn't it early in the day for a baseball game?" I asked.

Mr. A. tossed me a pretzel. "I tape them the night before 'cause I can't stay up past eight-thirty anymore.

If either of you know the final score, keep it to yourself. I haven't even read the morning paper or watched the news yet, just in case."

Ralph and I shook our heads simultaneously, and Mr. A. eased back into his chair, satisfied that we weren't about to ruin his game.

"You're as bad as a kid," Mrs. A. said when she returned a minute later with a plate full of gingerbread. She passed us each a pretty blue napkin. "Just in case," she smiled, pretending that she hadn't seen me spill crumbs all over her carpet a hundred times before.

Gingerbread in hand, I curled up next to their cat, Billy Duke. He was the fattest cat on the street. Ralph and I were sure he was the fattest cat in the world. I said that to Mr. A. once, but he said that Billy Duke wasn't overweight, just "big boned." I think he was trying not to hurt Billy Duke's feelings. I scratched the cat's ears and rubbed his tummy until he purred like an outboard motor, and then gave Mrs. A. the look I usually give her when I want to talk about something.

"What are you two up to?" she asked, settling herself into an empty chair.

"We're kind of working on something," I said.

"Goodness, that sounds important. Did you hear that, Burns? Tracy and Ralph are working on something."

One of the Yankees' players struck out and Mr. A. clutched his head. "I thought you were always working on something," he said. "Maybe this time your something could be something useful, like teaching the Yankees how to bunt."

Ralph frowned. "I'm not sure I follow you, Mr. Attwood. You want me to teach them how to make a cake?"

It was Mr. A.'s turn to look confused. "Who said anything about cake?"

Ralph turned to me for help. "Didn't he say he wanted me to teach them how to make a Bundt cake?"

Leave it to Ralph.

"Bunt, Ralph! Mr. A. wants us to teach the Yankees how to bunt!"

"Um, okay. Isn't that what I said?"

"I think you said Bundt, as in a German Bundt cake. Mr. A. was talking about the batter bunting a ball. You know—just hitting it gently so it only goes a couple of feet."

"Why would someone want to do that?" Ralph asked. "I thought batters are supposed to get home runs."

The Yankees' pitcher struck out a batter, and Mr. A. roared with delight. He looked across at Ralph. I was surprised when, instead of saying something smart to Ralph, he grinned. "It's all strategy, Ralph. Sometimes, it's better not to swing for the fences. It can be smarter to be gentle. But," he continued, his eyes returning to the TV, "I think the Yankees players would also benefit from learning to make Bundt cakes."

"What are you working on?" Mrs. A asked. I'd forgotten all about why we were there, thanks to the baseball conversation.

I smiled at her. "Have you seen anything weird over at the baseball field lately? I know you walk the track most evenings. It would probably have been a couple of nights ago."

"Twelve times every night. Good for the ticker," Mr. A. said, thumping himself on the chest.

"Doctor's orders," Mrs. A. added. "A couple of nights ago, right? What kind of weird thing?"

"Oh, you know, anybody hanging around the base-ball dugouts."

"Actually, something *was* going on over there the other night," Mr. A. said. "Remember, Tess? We said if one more person went over by those dugouts they were going to have to install a revolving door."

Mrs. A. giggled. "*That* night! You're right, Burns. It was wild!"

"Who did you see there?" I asked, taking a very large and unladylike mouthful of gingerbread, glad that Mom wasn't there to witness my greediness.

"Oh my goodness. I think the question is who *wasn't* there."

"Only the Munroes," Mr. A. said. "But that was only because you folks weren't home from Maine until the next day. Otherwise, I bet you would have all been there, too. Let's see. We saw Hazel McNutt's niece, Jasmine, with her friends, including the new kid who's moved in across the street—"

"Zach," I supplied.

"Yes, that's his name. And we saw Hazel, and Zach's father, Mr. Favorite—"

"Favola," Mrs. A. corrected her husband.

"Yes, yes, okay—Favola. And we saw our paperboy, Joe Tunney. Oh, and I think we saw you and Willie there, Ralph. Weren't you and Willie over there?"

I looked at Ralph. This was new information. "Why didn't you tell me you and Willie were at the baseball field?"

"Because we were only there for about three minutes. Willie forgot his water bottle in the other dugout," Ralph replied. He looked embarrassed.

"That's a lot of people," I said.

Mrs. A. passed me another piece of gingerbread. "It *was* a lot of people. We thought it was quite funny. Of course, they weren't all there at the same time. It usually takes us an hour and a half to walk three miles on a hot evening, and that night was especially hot. We take lots of breaks and drink lots of water. But why all the questions? Did something happen?"

I didn't want to lie to Mrs. A. She was one of my best friends on the street. "We've heard a rumor that someone lost something in one of the dugouts. Did it look like anybody was searching for anything?"

Mrs. A. shook her head. "Not that we noticed. Sorry we can't be more of a help."

"Actually, you were a big help," I said, smiling. "At least I know who was and wasn't there." I gave Ralph a meaningful look. He pretended to watch the game.

"*You* didn't go over by the dugouts, did you, Mr. A.?" Ralph asked. I was mortified that he would ask the Attwoods that, but they simply laughed in response.

"Sorry, old man," Mr. Attwood said. "We did not."

As we stood up to leave, Mr. A.—his eyes never leaving the television screen—added, "And next time you crawl in through my barn window, make sure you close it up tightly afterward."

Ralph and I gave each other a flustered look, mumbled our apologies, thanked Mrs. A. for the snacks, and fled.

"Maybe we aren't as sneaky as we think we are," Ralph said as we stumbled down the front walk.

"Or at least, *one* of us isn't," I replied.

CHAPTER 10

"Why didn't you tell me before that you and Willie were over at the dugout the night before last?" I asked as we crossed the street. "That could have been the night the money was left there."

Ralph stopped when we reached my driveway. He looked defensive. "I knew I didn't hide money in that dugout. I wasn't even in *that* dugout. Like I said, we went to the other one for a few minutes and then we left. I guess I didn't see the point of telling you useless information. Plus, we have no evidence that the money was left that night. We're only guessing."

"The point is we can't keep secrets from each other. Not if we're a team."

"I know, I know. Forget it, okay?"

As we walked up my driveway, the only sound was the gravel under our feet. I was thinking about how great it had felt to upset Jasmine earlier. I hadn't planned on meeting Zach again. Maybe now I should. I don't know what Ralph was thinking about. I hoped it was cooking. That made him happy. We were almost to the house when Lester suddenly popped out of the kitchen door.

"Howda go?" he asked, his words garbled and thick.

"We didn't find out who the money belongs to, if that's what you're asking," I replied. "How'd you make out at the dentist?"

"Painleth, but me mouff feelth full of cotton."

"You look like a chipmunk," Ralph said, pointing at Lester's chubby cheeks. "You know what? It's a good look for you. I'm going to start bringing you more of my baking."

"Thankth," Lester said. "Maybe I could liff weighths, too. Bulk up."

Lester hadn't meant to be funny, but as I looked from him to Ralph, I cracked up. And then Ralph cracked up, too, and we were both laughing hysterically. I laughed so hard that tears ran down my cheeks, making big wet stains on my T-shirt and skirt. Ralph laughed so hard he dropped to the ground, holding his ribs. Meanwhile, Lester watched us, confused.

"I don't underthtand whath's so funny," he said finally.

"I don't underthtand whath's so funny, either," Ralph gasped.

"But ith very funny," I added.

Lester rolled his eyes. "You guyth think I talk funny."

"Whatever gave you that idea?" Ralph said, trying to get a hold of himself. "My belly hurts from laughing so hard."

"Laugh all you like," Lester said, "but I thought we were thupposed to do a thtakeout over at the batheball field?"

That started us off all over again.

Finally, I wiped my eyes. "I'm sorry, Lester. You just sound so funny. You're right—we're supposed to go do a stakeout over at the ball field." I held my hand out to Ralph to help him up. "Think you're calm enough to go?"

"I think so," Ralph said. He put his arm around Lester's shoulder. "You made my day." Lester beamed.

Several minutes later, we emerged from the woods onto the ball field. I headed directly for the dugout, then stopped. Jasmine's sidekicks, Tanya Maslany, Tina Inoue, and Tiffany Brentwood, were sprawled across the wooden bench like abandoned rag dolls. Without thinking, I stepped back and bumped into Ralph and Lester.

"What do you think?" I muttered to Ralph. I wanted him to say 'Let's forget about it.' As far as I was concerned, these were the stupidest girls in town. The thought of trying to talk to them, to give them *any* of my attention, made me wary. We'd have to use small words to make sure they could understand and ignore their hyena-like tendencies when it came to laughing and trying to feed off the weakness of others. Even if we were friendly, they would not be. Why bother?

Ralph pressed his lips together for a moment, and then exhaled. "We don't have a choice. We've gotta see if they know anything."

I cracked my knuckles and we moved toward them.

Only when we were almost to the dugout did I realize we hadn't made a plan about how we'd question them. I regretted that as soon as Lester opened his mouth.

"Hi girlth," he said, trying to sound casual and cool. Instead, he sounded like a chipmunk with a speech impediment. The three Ts fell all over themselves in fake gales of laughter.

When they finally got themselves under control, Jasmine's second-in-command, Tanya, took the lead: "Can we, like, help you?"

I nudged Lester to let me do the talking. I hoped that his goofiness had gotten them to lower their guard.

"Hey, Ts. I was just wondering if you guys have seen anything odd today."

Tanya snorted and flipped her perfectly curled hair off her shoulders. It was as though she were flicking my comment away like an annoying mosquito.

"Except for you and your baby brother?"

They fell all over themselves again in hysterics, as though Tanya were a famous comedian. The only thing funny about her was the stupid-colored bands she had attached to her braces. I waited a minute and tried again.

"Whatever, Tanya. Then, the answer is no?"

Tanya sat up and smoothed down her too-short dress. She pointed back over my shoulder. "There's him. He's been hanging around *all* day. He keeps looking at us. I hope he doesn't have a crush on me. As if I would *ever* date him."

I turned to see who she was pointing toward. Joe Tunney was running the track again. Either he was going to try out for the track team when school started again, or he was keeping an eye on the dugout. My detective instincts told me it was option two.

"Joe's a good guy," Ralph said.

I expected Tanya to say something smart, but she merely shrugged. "If you say so, Ralph."

I could never tell if the Ts were nicer to Ralph because they knew it bugged me or if they actually kind of liked him.

"Nobody else?" I asked.

Tina shook her head. "I'll tell you the truth if it means you'll get lost. We haven't been here very long and we haven't seen anyone but Joe. Satisfied?"

"I—"

"You forgot. We ran into Zach," Tiffany butted in.

"Oh, right. And then he and Jasmine went to the store together," Tanya confirmed.

I was about to say thanks so that we could leave behind the cheap perfume cloud that hung over the dugout like some horrible pesticide spraying program gone bad when I realized it was no longer just the six of us. Jasmine was slithering out of the woods.

"I see you're bugging the Ts now, Tracy," she remarked in that snooty voice she likes to use when she wants to make someone feel stupid. I'm usually able to ignore it because I know I'm at least as smart as she is, but sometimes it gets under my skin. This was one of those times.

I spun around. "We were asking your friends a simple question. Not that it's any of your business."

Jasmine studied her friends' faces. She waved her hand dismissively and laughed. Only it wasn't a nice laugh like Ralph and I'd shared. It was cold and mocking. "You don't have to answer any of her questions, you know. It's not like she's the police or anything. It's just nosy old Tracy Munroe. Remember when she used to pretend she was a *detective?*" She said *detective* like it was a curse. The Ts giggled in their evil stepsister way.

I could feel myself bristling. "No one said we were the police."

"Then why are you asking questions about what people have been up to?" Jasmine asked. "Are you trying to get somebody in trouble?"

My mind raced as I tried to figure out how Jasmine could possibly know we'd been asking people questions.

As if she could read my mind, she added with a sneer, "Mr. Brown told Zach and me you were asking if anyone had lost anything."

"So what?"

"We're jutht invethstigating for fun," Lester said.

"Not helpful, Lester," I muttered.

Jasmine shrugged. "I don't know what you're investigating, but I'm sure it's something stupid. I thought maybe you were throwing yourself at my friends like you were throwing yourself at Zach earlier."

"She wasn't throwing herself at Zach," Ralph said, glaring. "*He* asked *her* if they could meet later. The only person I saw throwing themselves at Zach was you."

I knew how much that had cost Ralph to say, and I was grateful. Score one for our side.

"Whatever." Jasmine crossed her arms and looked at Ralph with contempt. "I think he likes girls who, well, look normal. Not like they got dressed out of their grandmother's closet."

I had a burning desire to reach over and yank on Jasmine's hair, which I was pretty sure had extensions in it but, instead, I turned and began walking toward the woods. All I wanted to do was go home. Ralph and Lester trailed after me. "*Whatever* is right," I said. "Not every guy likes fakes, Jasmine," I said loudly over my shoulder.

"What did you say?" she called out to our receding backs.

"She said: not evy guy likeths fakeths!" Lester shouted. He gave me a satisfied nod.

I could hear the Plastic Posse's laughter as we walked on. I decided not to tell Lester that Jasmine and the Ts would probably never let me live his swollen-mouth comment down. They'd be lisping at me every time they saw me until I did something else they could make fun of me for. I knew Lester meant well but, coupled with how weird he'd acted the day before around Zach, he was kind of becoming a liability.

♀ ♀ ♀

As soon as Ralph went home, I hid in my room, bringing Charlie with me for moral support. Flopping on the bed, I stared up at the ceiling and tried to make sense of the day. I'd only been home for a day, but it felt like our trip to Old Orchard Beach was months ago, what with the drama of finding the money, the drama of Ralph not liking Zach, and the drama of Hazel and Jasmine being mean to me about Zach for no reason. It was a lot to deal with at once.

One thing especially bothered me: Jasmine's comment about me dressing like my grandma. I wasn't sure why it bugged me so much. Maybe because I was already thinking about how Zach's style was almost identical to hers. Maybe he thought I dressed like someone's grandma, too. Until today, I'd never cared whether people liked the clothing I wore. But the idea of someone from New York City, someone cool like Zach, not liking my style was different. I wanted him to think I looked like I belonged in a big city.

I sighed dramatically, and Charlie glanced up. Normally, I would be able to talk about this stuff with Ralph, but he'd made that impossible. Why did Ralph have to dislike Zach so much? For the first time since Ralph and I had become friends, we didn't agree about someone, which made me feel queasy and a little afraid. Even worse, for the first time in forever, Jasmine and I had something in common: Zach.

If I was being honest, the fact that Jasmine was tangled up in all of this was the worst. She was always out to get me. Her comment about my clothing made me worried. It would be just like Jasmine to tell Zach I had a crush on him. I knew I didn't, but what if he thought I did? That would be the Worst. Thing. Ever. I'd have to go into hiding in a convent like Julie Andrews in *The Sound of Music* and I'd never be able to talk to Zach again because I'd be so mortified. Which was what she wanted, wasn't it? Jasmine didn't want me to hang out with Zach because she wanted him all to herself. I closed my eyes. All I could see was that awful smirk she'd given me at Brown's Store and in front of her friends. I'd do anything to wipe that smirk off her face. *Could I?*

I sat up. Why not? All I needed to do was make Zach like me more than he liked Jasmine. How hard could that be? I just needed to approach it like I approached a school test. There had been plenty of times in the past when I wasn't sure I'd come out on top, but with a little hard work, I'd always managed to get a good grade, often the best grade. For sure I could beat Jasmine at this, too. A plan started to percolate in my head. Zach and Jasmine had the same kind of trendy style. It wasn't going to be easy or natural, but I had to have that style as well.

Hopping out of bed, I ran to the mirror. Unlike Jasmine and the Ts, I wasn't allowed to wear makeup yet—not even lip gloss. And nothing would make my pasty skin look "sun-kissed" like the girls in the magazines. I couldn't even count on my hair. After wearing a hat for most of the day, it was a strange combination of tangled curls and weird flat pieces. Until that moment, I'd never thought about whether I was pretty or not. Scratch that. I'd never *cared* if I was pretty or not. I only cared about looking my own version of stylish and about getting good grades. After a few minutes of intense looking, I decided that even though I wasn't flashy, I had a certain something. Best of all, I had imagination. And imagination was going to beat Jasmine Singh.

I threw open my closet door. There wasn't much to work with if I wanted to try and look trendy. I ignored the reproachful look from the life-sized poster of Humphrey Bogart that was tacked to the wall nearby. "Don't look at me like that. It's all part of a plan," I told him.

I was sure Jasmine had no idea who Humphrey Bogart was. As far as I knew, Ralph and I were the only kids in our school who were fans of old movies, especially ones starring Bogey. I sighed. Zach wouldn't know who he was, either. But that was okay. I could tell him.

I pulled out my brightest red sundress and sprayed some sparkles in my hair and on my cheeks. Good, but not enough. I needed more *oomph*. I peeked out the door, checking for signs of Pig Face. The coast was clear. As stealthily as a jewel thief, I snuck into the bathroom and pulled open the drawer of the vanity where Mom stored her makeup. I stared at the neat rows of lipstick, the tubes of foundation and mascara, the small stack of eye shadows. I had no idea how to use any of it. But really, how hard could lipstick be? I grabbed the brightest color I could find and ran back to my room. Then, just like I colored in maps during social studies class, I scribbled the red on my pale lips. I tried to go slow and stay within the lines, cleaning my mistakes with Kleenex as I went.

I looked at myself in the mirror again. Except for the odd smudge of red on my face—which I quickly fixed by spitting on a Kleenex and rubbing again—I looked good. Actually, I looked glamorous, like I'd just stepped out of an old movie. Someone who didn't know me might mistake me for being twenty years old, thanks to the red lips.

I caught sight of Charlie staring at me as I looked at my reflection. I puckered my lips at her. She looked unimpressed.

In response, Charlie rolled over and went to sleep. Not exactly the effect I'd hoped for. But that was okay. I just needed to impress Zach.

Once I did that, Jasmine was toast.

CHAPTER 11

"Some Pig," Lester said to no one in particular. It was early afternoon the next day. Ralph had called us over for a detective team meeting and to taste test his latest brownie recipe.

"Excuse me?" I said. I'd barely been listening to his nonstop nattering as we made our way to Ralph's. I was distracted. Applying makeup had been harder than I'd thought it would be and even my untrained eyes could see that a person wasn't supposed to use that much blush. I'd been just as heavy-handed with the sparkle spray I'd put in my hair and the smell was giving me a headache. Worst of all, I'd borrowed a pair of high heels from Mom's closet and could barely keep my balance, wobbling from side to side. My mind was a muddle of missing money, getting Zach to like me more than he liked Jasmine, and how uncomfortable I felt dressed like this. The whole Marilyn Monroe thing was not working for me. And now Lester was talking about *pigs?*

"I said *Some Pig.*" Lester carefully enunciated each word.

I stopped, put my hands on my hips, and glared down at him. "Lester, I have no earthly idea what you're talking about."

Lester grinned his best evil-genius grin. "You know: *Some Pig.* Like in *Charlotte's Web.*"

"Okaaay." I drew the word out slowly, still unsure where this was going.

"You look like some pig" was his simple, straightforward response.

"I look like *what?*" I squealed, sounding, unfortunately, a little piglike.

"You know how in the book Charlotte spins a web with *Some Pig* written in it so that people will think Wilbur is special?"

"Yeah . . ."

"All that sparkly stuff in your hair and that lipstick and those super high heels that Mom doesn't know you took from her closet remind me of someone who's trying to make people think she's special, that's all. I've never seen you dress like this before."

It was such a Pig Face thing to say. He was the pig, not me. Furious, I attempted to leave him in my wake, but the high heels were so wobbly that I tripped, only to be saved at the last second when Pig Face grabbed my arm. *Did I really look that bad?* I didn't ask the question, because I already knew the answer: a resounding yes. I swallowed hard, trying to stop the tears that were already forming. How was I going to be able to compete with Jasmine if I couldn't even walk?

"You think it looks bad."

Lester suddenly looked uncertain. He could see he'd offended me, but the fact that I hadn't yelled at him had clearly confused him.

"Not bad, just, you know, different. I need to get used to it."

I winced. *I must look bad*, I thought. I considered

going home to change but decided to see what Ralph thought. He would tell me the truth.

"A lot of girls in my grade dress like this," I said, staggering forward, cursing the invention of heels. It felt like I was balanced on stilts that might topple at any moment.

Lester nodded and matched my snaillike pace, step for awkward step. He even let me lean a hand on his shoulder. "Yeah, I guess they do," he said. "I just didn't think you were like most girls."

Ouch. I was about to say something snarky when a movement caught my eye from the yard across the street.

"Did you see that?" I whispered.

Lester looked around. "See what?"

"At your nine o'clock, behind the shed over there."

"At my what?" he said, too loudly.

"Nine o'clock is a direction," I said. "You know, like the position of the hands on a clock."

"Ohhh . . ." Then, "You mean did I see Joe Tunney behind the shed? The answer is yes, I did. He's been following us for the past few minutes."

Joe had been following us and Lester hadn't thought to mention it? I stopped again, leaned over from my great altitude, and put my face very close to Lester's, so close that I could smell the Kraft Mac & Cheese he'd eaten for lunch on his breath. "You didn't think it was a good idea to tell me?"

Lester shrugged. "I thought you saw him, too."

I sighed and then lurched toward the shed, creeping as stealthily as I could in Mom's stupid ankle-breaking heels. But by the time I hobbled around back, Joe was gone. He must have realized he'd been spotted. I teetered back to Lester.

"You know this makes him the prime suspect," I said. "I bet he's figured out we have the money and he wants it back."

"How would Joe Tunney have fifteen hundred dollars? And why doesn't he just ask us for it if it's his?"

"Duh, because he stole it, that's why!" By now we'd reached Ralph's house. "Next time tell me when you see someone following us, okay?"

"Okay." As Lester stepped through the door after me, I swore I heard him mumble, "Some Pig."

ρ ρ ρ

Ralph was pulling the brownies out of the oven when we walked into the kitchen. He turned around, triumphant, and then stopped, frozen in place, his big oven-mitted hands squeezing the glass baking dish tightly. He looked me up and down, looked at Lester who shrugged, and then looked back at me. I waited for the inevitable comment, the cousin to Lester's "Some Pig," but nothing. Ralph placed the pan of brownies on the kitchen island, took off the oven mitts, and smiled.

"I think these are the best ones yet."

I couldn't decide if I was offended or relieved that Ralph had said nothing. In the end, I chose relieved. I smiled back, leaning over to pull the instruments of torture off my feet.

"What's the secret ingredient in these ones?" I asked. This was Ralph's tenth or eleventh attempt to perfect the brownie.

"Belgian chocolate," he said. "Mom bought it in Maine. I have high hopes."

"Belgian chocolate," I repeated. "Zach has chocolate

bars made of Belgian chocolate. They're called Dylan's Candy Bars. Have you heard of them?"

"I've read about them. How'd Zach get one? They don't sell them around here."

"His mom sent him a whole box of them. Apparently, he can't last the summer here if he doesn't have them."

"Too bad she sent them then," Ralph muttered. I gave him a look and he held up his hands.

"JK!" Lester looked at me confused and I mouthed "just kidding."

"Ha, ha. Where's your mom?" I asked, rubbing my feet and debating asking for a Band-Aid for the blister I could already see forming on my left heel.

Ralph looked at the clock. "She's still on her shift at the factory. Mrs. Mallory next door is keeping an eye on me. She just went home to put a load of laundry in. Willie's still at hockey camp—he won't be back for another four days."

"Yum," Lester's grubby paw reached for the pan but was intercepted by Ralph's oven mitt.

"They're still too hot to eat. They need to sit for ten

minutes before I can cut into them. We can discuss next steps in the investigation while we wait." Ralph waved the oven mitt over the pan to help with the cooling. "I sort of feel like we don't have a real plan yet."

"Well, Joe Tunney has something to do with the money," I said, leaning over to blow on the pan myself. The aroma was amazing and I was willing to do whatever was necessary to hurry things along.

"Joe Tunney! Why do you say that? Because we saw him running the track?"

I shook my head. "We saw him running the track *twice*. More importantly, Lester and I spotted him following us on our way here."

"I don't believe it," Ralph said. "Are you *sure* he was following you?"

"He definitely was," Lester confirmed, though his mind was on more important matters. "Are the brownies ready yet?"

"Five more minutes," Ralph said. He looked down at the pan and shook his head. "I can't believe Joe has anything to do with the money. Maybe he was following you for some other reason."

"Yeah, maybe he likes your new shoes, Tracy," Lester suggested.

The look I gave my brother would have withered a mere mortal, but didn't appear to bother Lester one bit.

"Don't you think it's strange that we find money in the baseball dugout two days ago at the exact time Joe Tunney is running the track, and now, all of a sudden, he's following Lester and me? You have to admit, it's awfully shady," I said.

Ralph shook his head. "Or it's a coincidence. Joe's a hard worker. I ran into him a couple of weeks ago and he said he was saving money so his little sister could take dance lessons this fall. He just has his mom, like me and Willie, so money's tight sometimes. Joe delivers a hundred papers every day, mows lawns in the summer, and shovels driveways in the winter. He is definitely *not* a shady guy."

Lester handed Ralph the knife with a hopeful smile. "Ralph's right, Tracy—you keep looking for bad guys. I think we should keep trying to find out who the money belongs to."

"How do we do that, Pig Face? We've asked around."

Lester looked offended. "We could go to the police like I said we should do two days ago."

I sighed. I knew he was right, but I desperately wanted to be the one to solve the mystery. "What do you think?" I asked Ralph.

Without looking up, Ralph began to score the brownies into large squares. "How about this: we give it two more days. We'll check Facebook again, the papers, ask everyone we know—except our parents—if they've seen anything strange or if they've lost any money. If we haven't figured out who the money belongs to by the day after tomorrow, we'll tell our parents and turn the money over to the police. Agreed?"

I didn't like it, but I knew he was right. "Okay. And if somebody did steal the money, maybe they'll slip up. We should keep an eye out for somebody who's just gotten something expensive or who wants to buy something that costs a lot of money." Joe was saving to help his sister take dance lessons. I knew from the one miserable year I took ballet that those were pricey.

I suddenly remembered before I'd left on vacation Ralph telling me how desperate he was to buy a secondhand food processor. He'd been searching all the usual places online and every junk store in town, but couldn't find one he could afford. Would he be desperate enough to steal? He had said cooking was impossible without one, and I knew that he lived to cook, so maybe . . .

I shook my head violently.

"Are you okay?" Ralph asked, handing me a brownie. I nodded. No way was Ralph a thief. I had to get a grip.

Before I could take a bite, "Over the Rainbow" began to play on my cell phone. "Hello?"

"Sweetie, it's Mom. That boy from next door is here looking for you, again. When shall I tell him you'll be home?"

I could feel my cheeks burning. "Tell him I'm on my way," I said, my voice sounding high-pitched and silly, even to me. I pressed Off and turned to Ralph.

"I gotta go," I said. "Zach—"

"I heard." Ralph cut me off. "You're just going to take off to go hang out with *him*?"

I hadn't told Ralph about my plan to beat Jasmine yet, and I definitely didn't want to tell him in front of

Lester. To be honest, I didn't want to tell him. He'd be upset. My anger toward Jasmine had me dressing like a reality TV star, and had me getting a guy who Ralph couldn't stand to like me better than her. Really, there was no good way to explain this plan, so I'd decided not to. "I'm not taking off. I'm seizing the opportunity to go talk to him and see what he knows."

"I thought you said Zach probably didn't know anything because he doesn't know anybody in town," Ralph said, crossing his arms.

"What do you want me to say? You were right and I was wrong. I forgot that he hangs out with Jasmine and the Ts. He could know something. We just said we'd talk to everybody. And I'm not blowing you off. You and Lester can come with me."

Ralph's shoulders relaxed a bit and he took a big bite of brownie, shaking his head. "No thanks. Maybe Lester and I will go see if we can find Joe."

"That would be awesome!" Lester said. "You and me, working together! Just like Batman and Robin!"

"Something like that," Ralph said, smiling.

Relieved that they weren't coming with me, I

sounded higher-pitched than normal when I responded. "That's a great idea. You guys do that, I'll talk to Zach, and we'll meet up later."

Ralph wrapped a brownie in a paper towel and handed it to me. "For your mom."

"You and I should bring some for the road, too, huh Ralph?" Lester suggested.

Ralph laughed. "Maybe I should get a container. I said I wanted to fatten you up."

Meanwhile, I put the cursed shoes back on my feet and wiggled my way to the door, trying to ignore the sounds of laughter coming from behind me. Once I was outside and out of sight, I pulled the shoes off in disgust and ran all the way home in my bare feet.

♀ ♀ ♀

Zach was waiting on the front steps again.

"Hey," he said, "that was fast."

I didn't know if I should pretend to act offended or thrilled, so I simply smiled and tried to seem mysterious, since I was pretty sure that's what Jasmine would do. I sat down on the front steps, crossing my legs casually, but when I did, I noticed my feet were filthy from the walk home and quickly uncrossed them again. Then I leaned forward and tried, with as much dignity as I could muster, to put my mother's shoes back on my feet. But they wouldn't slide on. My feet had swelled in the summer heat. After a few evil-stepsister-like tries I finally gave up. I was a disaster.

"How are you?" Zach asked. Not "you look nice" or "love the shoes." I'd gone to all that effort and nearly crippled myself, and all I got was a "How are you?" Zach was looking at me, but he wasn't really seeing me. Through an open window, I could hear Mom puttering around in the kitchen, and it was all I could do not to hop up and go join her and avoid the misery of sitting beside some boy who I'd failed to impress.

"I'm good, I guess." Dressing like Jasmine was not going to work. I'd have to find another way.

Before I could say anything else, my eyes began to water, thanks to the stupid mascara. Instinctively, I reached up and rubbed them, then instantly regretted it. More mascara goop slipped into my eyes, which began to burn.

I took a breath. What would Audrey Hepburn do in

a situation like this? *She'd pretend nothing was wrong,* I thought. I squared my shoulders and tried to act dignified.

Zach still didn't seem to notice my attempts to be alluring and refined. "Your mom said you were over at Ralph's. What were you guys up to?" He leaned a little closer, nudging my arm.

"Ralph made brownies—" I began, but Zach's snort cut me off. "Don't laugh! He's a great cook. He's going to be a famous chef when he grows up."

Zach held up his hands. "Is the amazing smell one of his brownies?"

I'd forgotten I was still holding the paper towel-wrapped treat. "Yeah, he sent one home for my mom."

Zach reached over and took the paper towel bundle out of my hand. Before I could grab it back, he'd unwrapped the brownie. "This smells so good it's making my mouth water. Maybe if I try it you'll convince me that Ralph is a good cook. Besides, your mom doesn't even know he sent one over for her. I won't tell if you don't." I began to protest but he laughed and took a huge bite, closing his eyes and chewing slowly, savoring every crumb of the treat he'd just stolen. *Ralph will go nuts if he finds out about this*, I thought. *And so will Mom.*

"That," Zach said, licking the last bit of chocolate off his right index finger, "was the best brownie I've ever eaten. Ralphie-boy can cook."

I debated giving Zach grief for stealing Mom's brownie, but I didn't want to argue with him. He'd leave and that would be the end of my plan to get back at Jasmine. I wondered what they talked about when they were together. Probably clothes and some silly show she watched on TV.

Then I remembered that I had actual interesting news I could share. "We're trying to solve a mystery," I blurted out.

"A mystery?" Zach looked impressed.

Now I had his attention. "Yeah, Ralph and I found a paper bag filled with money in one of the baseball dugouts a couple of days ago. We're trying to figure out who it belongs to." I leaned in closer. I didn't want Mom to overhear. I could smell the chocolate brownie on Zach's breath. "We think the money might have been stolen," I whispered.

"Stolen?" Zach said. "Wow."

"I know, right? We're following leads, trying to figure out who left it or lost it."

"Why haven't you called the police or put up notices?" Zach asked.

Now was my chance to really impress him. "We don't need the police. We're going to solve the mystery ourselves."

"Cool."

"Do you know Joe Tunney?" When I got a nod from Zach I kept going. "He's been acting kind of suspicious. He's my prime suspect."

Zach looked intrigued. "Suspicious? How?"

"He just seems to be around a lot, watching." I remembered Joe's shadow slipping behind the shed, and shivered.

"Huh. I haven't noticed Joe hanging around. It's pretty boring in this neighborhood. Ralph's been at Hazel's a few times, and Jasmine's friends were around a lot last week, but that's it."

"What was Ralph doing with Hazel?" As soon as the words came out of my mouth I felt like I'd betrayed my best friend. If I wanted to know what Ralph was up to, I owed it to him to ask him myself.

Zach shrugged. "I don't know. And Hazel wouldn't say. But it's kind of mysterious, don't you think?"

I nodded. It was more than *kind of mysterious*. It was making my stomach ache.

"This mystery solving sounds cool, though. I'd love to help."

I could hear the resounding no from Ralph and Lester. But Zach might have some good ideas. And it would bother Jasmine if he hung out with us. Bothering Jasmine was the plan, wasn't it? Maybe I couldn't beat Jasmine when it came to acting like some gooey girl, but as a smart detective? No problem.

I shouldn't have thought of her, because there she suddenly was, standing in Hazel's front yard as if I'd conjured her. She waved wildly at Zach and walked in our direction, moving like a heat-seeking missile. Jasmine hadn't stepped foot in my yard since my fifth birthday, and while it must have pained her to do so now, she marched up the front walk, a determined look on her face.

"Hi, Zach!" she called, then added a half-hearted "Hi, Tracy" at the last minute.

"Hi, Jasmine," Zach said. He looked extremely pleased to see her. I looked extremely displeased and gave her a curt nod.

"I was looking for you, Zach," she said, resting one hand on her hip, carefully arranging herself in the most graceful position she could. I tried my best to hide my dirty feet. Jasmine looked freshly ironed, not a hair out of place. Even her toenails were painted a pretty pink.

"What's up?" Zach asked.

"Aunt Hazel just offered to take us to supper with her later this afternoon at one of the nice restaurants in St. Andrews."

"Where's that?"

"It's about twenty minutes away, beside the ocean."

"Will I be able to try lobster?" he asked.

Jasmine giggled. "Aunt Hazel says the restaurant has the best lobster in New Brunswick."

"I'm in!"

Jasmine flashed me a triumphant smile. "Sorry to

steal him away from you, Tracy." She glanced down at Mom's abandoned shoes, which were resting beside my feet. "Nice kicks."

I vowed to never wear them again.

"You're not stealing him away from me," I said. "I've got stuff to do anyway." My dad says you never want your opponent to see you sweat. Jasmine smiled, triumphant. I knocked her down to size with my next comment: "But I wouldn't mind talking to him alone for a couple more minutes." The smile vanished, replaced by a scowl, but she managed to hold herself together and nodded.

"No problem. Zach, before we go, Hazel asked if we could run a few errands for her, so come over as soon as you can, okay? Oh, and Tracy . . ."

I waited for the other shoe to drop.

"You definitely need to wash your face. You've got serious raccoon eyes going on." She grinned wickedly and turned away. If I'd wanted to hide under a rock before, now I wanted to hide under the Big Rock. I was pretty sure I didn't want to know what my face looked like.

Zach remained oblivious to my trauma. "So can I be part of the mystery-solving team?"

"Maybe . . ." I tried not to sound as cautious as I was feeling.

"C'mon," he pleaded. "Think of the fun we'd have." He leaned forward again and looked into my eyes. My whole face flamed with embarrassment and exhilaration.

"I'd have to check with the others," I said.

Zach looked glum. "Don't bother. Ralph will just say no. It's too bad. I watch all kinds of detective shows on TV. Just last month, my mom took me to a film festival and we saw Humphrey Bogart play a detective, Sam, Sam—"

"Sam Spade," I supplied. He *did* know who Humphrey Bogart was! I took that as a sign.

"Yeah, it was so cool. You gotta let me help you guys."

I wanted Zach to help us, not just because of Jasmine, but because I was sure he'd have some good ideas.

An idea popped into my head. It was sneaky and Ralph would be furious if he found out, but he didn't need to find out, did he?

I smiled at Zach. "Okay, you can help, but you can't tell Ralph or Lester that you're working with me. It has to be our secret."

Zach held up his right hand. "I promise I won't tell anyone," he said, then nudged me gently with his shoulder, like I was his new best friend.

We sat smiling at each other for a good ten seconds before Mom ruined the moment by opening the front door. We turned and looked up at her. She had a funny look on her face, and Charlie, who was standing in the doorway beside her, gave Zach the evil eye. "Lester just called. He wanted you to know that they're back at Ralph's. He says you have a brownie for me." She saw the balled-up paper towel and looked disappointed. "A brownie that I see you've eaten."

"My fault," Zach said, standing up and smiling at Mom. "I couldn't resist."

Normally, my mom is nice to everyone. Not this time. Zach had gotten between her and her brownie. She looked Zach up and down and shook her head. "I'm sure it *was* good. I'll ask Lester to bring me another."

As she turned to go back inside, she stopped to look

at me. "I think you'd better come in now, Tracy. I need help with something."

I was going to ask what she needed help with but it didn't matter. Zach was already halfway down the walk.

"See you later?" I called to his receding back.

"Sure thing, kid," he called, not bothering to turn. "Let me know when you're ready to start on the case."

"Thanks a lot, Mom," I said as I followed her into the kitchen.

Mom kept her eyes straight ahead. "You are most welcome. Please put my shoes back in my closet and then go wipe off that lipstick and the rest. You know you're not allowed to wear makeup." I waited for her to give me more grief and was surprised when she went back into her office.

As I climbed the stairs, a pang of guilt gripped me. I was keeping a big secret from Ralph and Lester. They would be furious if they found out.

But they weren't going to find out. I would make sure they wouldn't.

CHAPTER 12

Maybe I should have asked if I could go back over to Ralph's, see what he and Lester had found out, but I wanted to be alone to think about things for a while. After my conversation with Mom, I wandered from room to room, looking out the window, randomly picking up and then putting down knickknacks, feeling all jittery, like I imagined people must be when they've downed a full pot of coffee. Finally, I found myself in my bedroom, lying face up on the bed, staring at the ceiling. Again.

The thrill of my original plan to torture Jasmine like she always tortured me was wearing off. Sure, I was going to work with Zach to solve the mystery, but

Jasmine was going to supper with him. And my attempt to become a card-carrying member of the glamour squad had failed miserably. I hadn't even had the courage to take off the makeup yet because I was so terrified by what I'd see in the mirror.

I kept replaying the moment when I told Zach about the paper bag full of money, trying to find a good reason why I'd had no choice but to betray Ralph's and Lester's trust. There was none. Less than twenty-four hours before, I had glared at Lester when he'd almost given away the location of our secret lair. That was nothing compared to me blabbing about the money. I had messed up—big time. What would they do if they found out?

I got up the courage to go look at myself in the mirror. The Tracy in the reflection—wearing bright red lipstick and ghoulish mascara in an effort to look older and prettier—didn't look like me at all. How had I changed *so* much in such a short period of time? How had making Jasmine mad and impressing Zach become so important that I was willing to look like *this*? All of a sudden I wanted to rewind the clock, go back to being me. I missed me. I just couldn't figure out how to bring me back.

♀ ♀ ♀

I'd just finished cleaning the lipstick off when I heard the kitchen door open and close. I went to the top of the stairs and waited for Lester to call my name. Instead, I could hear Mom talking with someone, so I crept down the stairs and took a seat on the second to last step, the one that lets you hear everything that goes on in the kitchen, but lets you stay hidden.

"I haven't seen you in a while," Mom said, her words accompanied by the soft glug of mugs being filled.

"Oh, you know, I was busy getting the apartment ready, and then you folks were away, so this was my first chance to pop over."

Hazel McNutt! Wasn't she supposed to be going out to dinner with Zach and Jasmine?

As if she'd heard my thought, she added, "I had a few minutes to spare before I go to St. Andrews, so I thought I'd come over for a visit. I'm taking Jasmine and Zach Favola to the Algonquin Hotel for dinner. Zach wants to try Bay of Fundy lobster."

I leaned forward so I wouldn't miss anything.

"You're making me hungry," Mom said. Mom loves to go to the Algonquin Hotel for dinner. She thinks it's swanky. "I was going to ask how things were going with your new tenants, but if you're taking Zach to the Algonquin, I'd say they're going well."

"I think so, but actually, it was Jasmine's idea. She's sweet on the boy."

I knew it!

Mom said something I couldn't quite make out.

"Actually, I'm not even paying for the dinner. Jasmine's come into a little money and wanted to take me there as a thank you for letting her stay while her parents were out of town. She thought it would be fun if Zach came, too."

Jasmine had come into some money? Finally—a real clue!

"Lucky Jasmine," my mom said.

Lucky Jasmine my foot, I thought. *More like Jasmine the Crook.*

Hazel laughed. "It's too bad Zach's father can't come with us, but he's very busy at work. You know, we've gone on a couple of dates . . ."

I grabbed at my neck in mock disgust, remembering the picture of the two of them, and how Hazel called him her "Silver Fox."

"I'm happy you're dating again, Hazel."

Happy Hazel was dating again? Happy Hazel was inflicting herself on some poor, unsuspecting guy? Give me a break!

"Well it's just for the summer, but it's nice. To be honest, it's taken me a bit of time to warm up to Zach. But then, I've never had children, so I'm not used to them."

How could anyone not warm up to Zach? I thought of Ralph. How weird was it that neither Ralph nor Hazel liked him? Then it hit me—Ralph had been doing something for Hazel. Maybe Hazel had poisoned Ralph's mind against Zach! Poor Zach—it was bad enough that he was stuck living in Hazel's house for the summer and that she was dating his dad, but then she had to rob him of the chance to be friends with Ralph!

"Kids will be kids," Mom said, as if that explained everything. "Tracy's going through a thing this summer, too."

What? What kind of thing?

"You don't have to tell me about Tracy," Hazel snorted.

I leaned as far forward as I could go, holding the banister so I wouldn't do a face plant onto the hall floor.

"I don't know what you mean, Hazel." I could hear the worry in Mom's voice.

"I caught her letting your dog do its business on my lawn only a few hours after I'd had it fertilized. There was a sign on the grass and she completely ignored it."

I waited for Mom to defend me, to tell Hazel that dogs will be dogs. Instead, Mom just sighed. "I'm sorry, Hazel. I'm sure it was an accident."

Hazel made a huffing noise that reminded me of the Big Bad Wolf. I wished I could blow *her* house down. "Jasmine says that Tracy is trying to break up her friendship with Zach."

What! My shock was quickly replaced by euphoria. My plan was working!

"I think we should leave the kids to deal with their own friendships," Mom said.

I totally agreed. Hazel huffed again.

"I just don't want Jasmine to have her feelings hurt. She's a sensitive girl."

Jasmine Singh was as sensitive as a rattlesnake.

Mom sighed. "Kids need to learn on their own, Hazel."

"You're the mother, not me," Hazel said in a tone that made me think that she didn't think much of my mom's parenting skills. "But surely you don't agree that Tracy should sass me?"

Uh-oh. This wasn't going to end well.

"Tracy sassed you?" Now Mom wasn't sounding quite as sympathetic toward me. "What did she say?"

Hazel sniffed. "When I sent her home after you called the other day, she made a disparaging remark about my track record with men."

I didn't know what disparaging meant, but I knew it wasn't good.

"I'm so sorry, Hazel. That's unacceptable behavior. She's upstairs. I'll call her down to apologize. Tracy!"

I snuck back up the stairs so it would sound like I was coming down from my room, not eavesdropping from the bottom step. As I stomped back down the stairs, I began practising apologies in my head, each one more painful than the last. It seemed very *Anne of Green Gables*-ish to me and I began to feel "hard done by." When I walked into the kitchen, I gave Hazel a timid smile. I got nothing in return.

"Tracy, I—" Mom began, but I held up my hand.

"Excuse me, Mom. I have something to say to Hazel." Both Mom and Hazel steeled themselves. But I was as gooey and sticky as one of Ralph's cinnamon buns.

"Hazel, I'm so sorry about the other day. I should never have said anything about you and men, even if it was under my breath. It was a mean and stupid thing to say. I guess I was just embarrassed about what you said to *me* about Zach." I pretended to look shy so I could win her trust. The next part pained me to say, but I swallowed my pride. I needed to pull on Hazel's heart-strings. "You know, he's the first boy I've ever kind of liked." So what if this was a huge exaggeration?

Hazel said nothing at first. I could tell from the look on her face that she was weighing her possible responses. Finally, she settled on a warm, sympathetic smile. She felt sorry for me; just like I hoped she would.

"Never mind, Tracy. Women say funny things when they're in love."

Ugh. I wanted to protest, but now was not the time to argue with Hazel.

"I guess so," I said, giving her my best thank-you-for-being-so-understanding look. I glanced over at Mom. She didn't seem quite as moved by my apology.

"Regardless of the reason, Tracy, it is absolutely unacceptable to be rude, especially to an adult, and especially to a good neighbor and friend like Hazel. You're very lucky that she's accepted your apology."

"You're right," I said. I counted to three before I continued on. Timing was everything, after all.

"Can I ask you both a question?" I needed to turn the conversation away from me and back to something helpful, like information-gathering. "Have either of you seen anything out of the ordinary in the neighborhood during the past few days?"

"No, why do you ask?" Mom's tone was cautious. She'd watched my apology through the eyes of someone who had experienced my charms one too many times before and I could tell she knew I was trying to change the subject.

"I dunno. I heard someone might have lost something."

Mom shook her head. Hazel tilted hers and looked at me, like she was thinking.

"Hazel?" I prompted. I was sure I saw a flash of something cross Hazel's face, but then it passed and she shook her head.

Before I could say anything else, the Homer Simpson clock on the wall chimed "Doh! Doh! Doh! Doh!"

Hazel glanced down at her watch, wiped her mouth on her napkin, and stood up. "I've got to go home," she said. "It's almost time for me to take the kids to dinner. Thanks for the coffee, Pat," she said to Mom. She looked down at me. "Thank you for the apology, Tracy." And then Hazel was gone, leaving Mom peeved at me. But I was positive about one thing: Hazel McNutt knew something. But what?

CHAPTER 13

I ran up to my room and texted Ralph: **Where are you and Lester?**

Two seconds later, a beep: **At Big Rock.**

On my way, I texted back. It took me longer to get there because I was constantly looking over my shoulder, darting here and there, using all my stealthy maneuvers in case I was followed again. When I finally scrambled up the side of the Big Rock, I heard the crunching of peppermints before I even saw Ralph and Lester.

"Hey," I called as I came over the edge.

Lester glanced at my feet, now comfortably tucked inside a pair of Chucks. "Better shoes. And you look normal again without all that junk on your face."

I sat down beside him and gave him a shove. "How'd it go with Joe?" I asked.

Ralph shook his head. "We couldn't find him anywhere. I checked all the places he usually hangs out, tried calling and texting him. I even checked with his sister. But no luck. We came here to regroup." He looked at Lester. "Wait. Let me revise that. We came here after Lester stopped to go to the bathroom at home, and then again behind one of the old wrecks in the junkyard."

Lester held up his hands. "What? A guy's gotta go when he's gotta go."

"Lester! You can't go to the bathroom in public! That's gross! What if someone catches you?"

I received a shrug in response. Honestly, I was going to have to talk to my parents about this. What if it became a habit?

"Whatever, Lester. Listen guys. I've got news," I said.

"Thank goodness someone has something," Lester replied. "Ralph and I have nothing."

Ralph ignored him. "What did you find out?"

"Two things: one, Jasmine has suddenly come into some money and two, Hazel McNutt knows something!"

"Seriously?" Ralph sat up straighter.

"How do you know?" Lester asked.

"Hazel came over to have a cup of coffee with Mom. She told Mom that Jasmine was taking her and Zach to supper at the Algonquin Hotel tonight. For lobster."

Ralph whistled. "Do you know how much that would cost? A lot."

I nodded. "I know. The money could be Jasmine's."

"If the money is Jasmine's, it means it was probably just lost then, not stolen," Lester said.

"Maybe . . ." I wasn't prepared to let Jasmine off the hook. "But I have something else to tell you: when I asked Mom and Hazel if they'd heard of anybody losing anything, Hazel got a funny look on her face."

"I bet she realized Jasmine stole her money!" Lester crowed. "Yippee! We solved the case!"

"That doesn't make any sense, Lester," Ralph said, taking an extra loud crunch of his peppermint. "Hazel's not stupid. She said Jasmine came into money, not stole it. Did Hazel say she lost anything?"

I shook my head. "Not exactly. But the look on her face was strange."

"Are you sure it wasn't indigestion?" Lester joked.

"Ha, ha, ha. Very funny, Lester. No, it wasn't indigestion. I don't know what it was. But it was something."

"That's it?" Lester asked. He was starting to bug me, questioning everything I said.

"Yeah, but—"

"Lester's right, Tracy. It's not much to go on."

"You're supposed to agree with me, not him, Ralph!"

"I'm supposed to agree with what makes sense."

Lester stuck his tongue out at me and I shook my head in disgust.

"I saw what I saw," I countered, hopping to my feet. "I think Hazel might have lost the money."

Ralph and Lester looked up at me. It was clear they thought I'd gone bonkers.

"No, you guys listen to me! Hazel has a lot of money. She's always buying stuff, isn't she? Isn't it possible that she could have lost money and not even known if it was gone?"

Ralph shook his head. "Fifteen hundred dollars is a

lot of money to anyone, Tracy. I think you're stretching here."

"I'm not. Seriously, as soon as I asked the question, she got up and left."

"Maybe she had to go somewhere?" Lester said.

I remembered Hazel looking at her watch. I'd forgotten about that part. But I didn't want to tell Lester that. He'd never let me live it down.

"And I've never seen Hazel over at the ball field," Ralph said. "So how did the money get there? Did it walk there by itself and hide under the bench?"

Now they were making me angry. "Of course not. Someone stole it from her, duh. Maybe she's too embarrassed to say someone stole her money. Maybe she's protecting someone. In the movies, people are always protecting people they love from getting caught by the police and going to jail. Even Humphrey Bogart thought about protecting Mary Astor in *The Maltese Falcon*."

"But he didn't protect her in the end," Ralph said.

"No, but think about it: there are people coming and going from Hazel's all the time. The people who deliver packages to her, Jasmine and her friends, Joe Tunney—"

"Zach," Ralph added, raising an eyebrow and waiting for my reaction.

"You." I could give as good as he could.

Ralph flushed. "Are you saying you think *I* stole money from Hazel?" He clambered to his feet and began to pace the top of the rock, his hands raking his hair.

"Give me a break. Of course I don't think you took the money. We were just listing people that were around Hazel's house and you were one of them, weren't you?"

I waited to see if Ralph would finally tell me what he'd been doing at Hazel's while I was away. Instead, he continued to pace.

"Ralph wasn't around Hazel's place," Lester said.

"Yes, he was. Weren't you, Ralph?"

Ralph turned red. "I was, but I can't tell you why. I promised."

"Who'd you promise?" I asked. I had a vision of a witchy Hazel forcing him to do a blood oath.

"None of your business, that's who! I gave my word, and I'm not going back on it."

"Mom says that grown-ups shouldn't ask kids to make promises that make them keep secrets," Lester said.

"Give me a break, Pig Face," Ralph snapped, looking more and more like a rain cloud ready to burst. "Trust me: it's not a bad promise. And my mom knows all about it, so never mind saying stupid stuff like that."

Now I was dying to know what secret of Hazel's Ralph was keeping. It couldn't be dead bodies in the basement, because I was pretty sure Ralph's mom wouldn't be okay with that. I went through other possible options. Hazel needed Ralph to move all of her furniture so she could make room for more unopened boxes. Nah—that was hardly something Ralph would feel the need to keep secret. Of course, it might not be moving furniture at all, but Ralph was big and strong, so it made sense to me that Hazel would have him do something like that. Maybe Hazel was having Ralph move furniture because she and Mr. Favola were going to get married and she needed to make room for his things. Poor Zach! But then it hit me: if Zach's dad married Hazel, Zach would be coming to St. Stephen a lot. That would be awesome! And Ralph would learn to like him and the three of us would watch old movies and become best friends. I smiled at the thought.

Lester had reached up and was tugging at my arm. "Uh, Tracy?" Leave it to Pig Face to burst my happy bubble.

I looked down at my brother. "What?"

"I'm hungry. And we're getting nowhere with this Hazel stuff."

I looked over at Ralph. "Yeah, I'm done, too. I don't know what we do now. We only have one more day and then we have to go to the police."

"Let's watch Hazel's house like you said, and see if we see anything suspicious," Ralph said. "That's all I can think of. And I'll try and talk to Joe Tunney again. I still think he might have seen something. Sound like a plan?"

"I think I need to go—now," Lester said, and he trotted over to the far side of the Big Rock and peed over the edge into the bushes below.

"Good grief," Ralph said.

"What?" Lester adjusted his shorts as he walked back toward us. "It's the call of the wild, you know."

He came and stood beside me, but I stepped away from him. "You are so gross."

Lester blew me a kiss and went to reach for a peppermint. Ralph grabbed the bag in the nick of time. "No peppermints until you wash your hands. Tracy's right. You *are* gross."

My baby brother shrugged. "Whatever. Watch Hazel's house if you like, but I think we should keep talking to lots of people, not just Joe. Especially the people we know Mr. and Mrs. Attwood saw over at the ball field. By the way, you never told us what you found out from Zach, Tracy."

I blushed, thinking of how I'd told Zach about us finding the money. Why did my face always have to give me away?

Then I saw the suspicious look Ralph was giving me. He leaned down and looked me straight in the eye. "What happened?"

"What do you mean?" I asked.

Ralph's jaw clenched. "You know what I mean. Spill it."

Lester looked from me to Ralph, confused. "Spill what?"

Ralph's laugh was bitter. "Something happened. Didn't you see how she blushed when you said his name?"

Lester studied my face, looking for telltale signs of whatever it was Ralph was talking about. By now, my face was bright red with anger. I hated that Ralph always knew when I was hiding something. At least this time he had no idea how awful my secret was. I knew he just thought I liked Zach.

"He doesn't know anything, so you can stop with the drama, Ralph. I don't know why you dislike him so much. He's not a bad guy. What's he ever done to you, anyway?"

It was Ralph's turn to blush. "Nothing I want to talk about. C'mon, let's go. I promised Mom I'd make pancakes for supper."

I nodded and followed the two of them down the

side of the rock, through the woods, across the stream, through the junkyard, and along the train tracks. I didn't say a word the entire way, but my mind was going a hundred miles an hour.

I regretted telling Ralph and Lester that I thought the money might be Hazel's. I had no proof except for the strange look I'd seen on Hazel's face. We were turning out to be busts as detectives. Unless something happened soon, my dream of being a hero was never going to happen.

♀ ♀ ♀

After dinner, I plunked myself down in a lawn chair in the backyard with a pad of paper and a black marker. I'd decided to work on the suspect list before we met Ralph the next day. I drew two long lines on the page so that there were three columns. At the top of the first, I wrote NAME, and at the top of the second and third, I wrote PRO and CON. I needed to think things through logically. Seeing the facts on paper helped. I knew Ralph would be impressed with my chart when

I showed it to him. I was so focused on the first name on the list, Jasmine's, that I didn't notice that Zach was standing beside me until he spoke.

"What's up?" His voice was a lazy drawl.

I stared up at him. In the evening light he looked kind of golden. "I was just working on the case," I said. My voice sounded higher to me again. "How was dinner?"

"Awesome. I ate a lobster that was caught this morning. Isn't that cool? I took a picture and texted it to my mom." He pulled out his cell phone and thumbed through his pictures until he found the one of a good-sized lobster sitting on a bed of lettuce on a fancy plate. It was the first time I'd heard Zach sound excited since I'd met him. He thumbed to the next picture, which was of Jasmine and Hazel wearing lobster bibs and big smiles. I tried not to gag.

"Your dad couldn't go with you?"

Zach made a face. "He was too busy working. That's all he does. I don't know why he wanted to bring me here. I never see him. Tomorrow I start doing yard work and odd jobs for people I don't even know. He didn't even give me a choice. He says if he hears I'm slacking at all he's going to ground me. As if being stuck in this boring town isn't grounding enough."

"St. Stephen is not a bad town."

"Sorry, I didn't mean to rag on St. Stephen. I just miss home and my mom, ya know."

I couldn't help but feel a little sympathetic. I'd missed St. Stephen a lot when we were away. "It's too bad your dad's giving you such a hard time."

"Yeah, well, that's my dad." Zach leaned over to peek at the list. He saw Jasmine's name and winced.

"Why do you think Jasmine has something to do with the money you found?"

It took me a second to come up with a diplomatic response that wouldn't offend him. "I'm just putting everyone that was seen at the ball field on the list, that's all."

"Jasmine's too nice to steal money."

You sure don't know Jasmine, I thought.

"Plus, I questioned her when we were running errands for Hazel this afternoon." When he saw the worried look on my face, he held up a hand. "No, it's okay. I didn't tell her that I was working with you, but I did ask enough questions that I'm convinced she's not the thief."

I wasn't convinced, but I kept my mouth shut.

"What about the Ts?"

"I asked her about them, too. Apparently, Tiffany stole a chocolate bar from Brown's Store once."

Tiffany Brentwood had shoplifted? I almost fell out of the lawn chair in surprise. "Did she get caught?" I asked breathlessly. I couldn't wait to tell Ralph.

"Yeah. Mr. Brown called her parents and she had to return the chocolate bar and write him a letter apologizing."

"Wow! She must have been mortified!"

"Jasmine said she cried for a week. So she's positive that Tiffany will never steal again for as long as she lives. She won't even set foot in Brown's Store anymore. She makes the other girls go in and buy what she wants."

I wrote down Tiffany's name, made a couple of points in her pro and con columns, and looked back up at Zach. "Anything else?"

"Nope. That's all I found out. How about you?"

"I have a theory about who the money belongs to."

Zach's eyes lit up. "You do? Who?"

"Hazel."

"No way." Zach looked troubled. "She never mentioned losing money to me. And for sure she never mentioned it to my dad or he would have been all over me, giving me the third degree. Did she say who she thinks took it?"

I began to backtrack a little. "She didn't exactly say she'd lost any money."

From the look on Zach's face, I could tell he thought my hunch was dumb.

"We need facts," he said. His eyes traveled up and down my list. "I bet it's the paperboy. He's always creeping around over at the field."

I knew Zach was going to prove helpful. "I agree!" I said, feeling animated again. "Lester and I are sure he was following us earlier this afternoon."

Zach pointed to the paper. "Add that to the list of pros for him. Meanwhile, I'll keep my eyes and ears open." Not waiting for a response, he turned and slipped back through the hedge to Hazel's yard.

I had just begun to review the list again when a loud voice fractured the quiet of the night. "I told you to mow Hazel's lawn twenty minutes ago!" The anger in the voice I was sure belonged to Zach's dad made me sit back in my chair, stunned.

"I was just talking to Tracy next door—" Zach began, but his father cut him off.

"I don't care if you were talking to the man in the moon. Get the work done. When a Favola says he's going to do something, a Favola does it. Now get going. I'll be out when you're done to inspect it."

Seconds later, I heard Hazel's back door slam. I kept my head down, pretending to concentrate on my work in case Zach looked back over. If my parents yelled at me like that in front of someone, I'd be mortified. Only when I heard the drone of the lawn mower, did I relax again.

I sighed. It was obvious that Zach really liked Jasmine. And I was pretty sure he liked her way more than he liked me. My plan to defeat her wasn't working.

Jasmine was winning—again. I looked down at the list and bit my lip. The mystery-solving wasn't going well either. I circled Joe Tunney's name. He was our man. Now I just had to prove it.

CHAPTER 14

The next morning Lester and I left the house early to meet Ralph at the ball field. This was a big day: we had to solve the mystery or give up our chance to be heroes, although I had the nagging feeling that the longer we had the money, the less likely it was that people would think of me and Ralph as the good guys. Still, I had dressed up especially nice—a long baggy T-shirt of my mom's that I'd belted and worn as a dress, my bright pink-striped Chucks, and a wide-brimmed straw hat that I was convinced made me look like I'd stepped out of an eighties movie.

Lester was cheerful the whole way to the field. "You see what I've got here?" he said, pointing to the small

Lord of the Rings knapsack he was in the process of unzipping. I stopped and leaned over to look. I knew if I didn't, he'd just keep bugging me until I did.

He began to pull things randomly from his Mary Poppins-like bag. For a small knapsack, it sure seemed to hold a lot of stuff. Each item had its own story, too. It was like some bizarre Pig Face inventory of all the things we might need to solve the mystery.

"A notebook and three pens. We may need to make notes and you never know when your pen might run out." I noticed that one of them was his precious NASA space pen he'd gotten when we visited Cape Canaveral last winter. Lester was taking solving this mystery seriously.

"Rope?" I asked as a long yellow coil that was supposed to be our new clothesline was pulled from the bag.

"A guy has to be prepared." He reached in again. "Walkie-talkies. We may need these."

"I have a phone," I pointed out. "Walkie-talkies are so yesterday."

"You may have a phone, but I don't yet—and thanks for reminding me by the way—so this is all I have to work with." He thrust one of the blue plastic transmitters in my hand. "We'll each have one. You know, in case we get separated."

"Why would we get separated?"

"You never know. I thought you were a Brownie. Be prepared, and all that."

"I don't think Brownies say that. Isn't that the Boy Scouts?"

Lester shrugged. "Just keep it, okay?"

"Fine." I stuck the walkie-talkie into the small leather purse I'd slung over my shoulder and leaned over to see what else he'd brought. He pulled the bag off to the side. It was clear he would reveal the contents at his own pace. But I was getting antsy. "Will this take much longer? Ralph's waiting for us."

"Only a couple of more things to show you." The rummaging continued. A bag of licorice was shoved aside so he could pull out a can of Silly String.

"Silly String?"

"It's the kid version of pepper spray. I was going to borrow the bear spray Dad takes with him when he goes fishing, but I couldn't find it. This was the next best thing."

"Weirdly logical." I was happy he couldn't find the bear spray. An image of him accidentally spraying me made my eyes water.

Then he pulled out a book.

"You brought a Hardy Boys mystery?"

"Not just *any* Hardy Boys mystery. *Hunting for Hidden Gold.*" He showed me the cover. In the picture, Joe and Frank Hardy were digging for something, and a menacing man was creeping up on them.

"Does Dad know you took one of his prized books?" My dad had been working for ten years to collect a complete Hardy Boys set. He's very nostalgic about Joe and Frank and the scrapes they get into.

Lester waved me off. "I thought it was cool. You know, 'cause you and Ralph kind of found hidden gold, too."

"Um, no. We found fifteen hundred and ten dollars in a paper bag."

"Whatever. I thought we could give our mystery

a name, you know, like *The Mystery of the Dugout Diamonds*."

"But we didn't find diamonds."

"Okay. How about *The Mysterious Bag of Doom?*"

"You had me until *doom*. Why don't you just call it *The Mysterious Paper Bag?* Why does our mystery need a name, anyway?"

Lester looked at me as if I were an idiot. "What are the newspapers going to call it? And *Bag of Doom* sounds a lot more exciting than calling it a plain old paper bag."

I wondered if Zach would think naming the mystery was cool or silly. Still, I liked the idea of a name. It would help people remember us.

Lester shoved the Hardy Boys book back into his knapsack. "And, finally, the *pièce de résistance*." He pulled out a pipe.

"Lester, why do you have a pipe?" Despite wanting to maintain an air of professionalism, I couldn't help but giggle at the sight of Lester standing there, an unlit pipe hanging from his mouth. He looked like a cartoon character.

"Glad you asked, Watson. It's elementary. Sherlock Holmes has a pipe so, therefore, Lester T. Munroe must have a pipe. I found it in the attic. When I showed it to Mom, she said it belonged to our great-grandfather." He pretended to puff away, but then suddenly began to cough violently. I slapped him on the back a couple of times, afraid he was choking.

"Are you okay?" I said when he finally caught his breath and could stand up straight again. He looked a little green around the gills.

"I think our great-grandfather forgot to empty his pipe," he gasped.

"Lester, Sherlock Holmes used a magnifying glass, too. Maybe you should bring *that* next time?" Lester still looked sick, but nodded. "Do you need your inhaler?" I asked.

He shook his head, threw the pipe back into the knapsack with a look of disgust, and then slung his portable detective office on his back. In seconds he'd gone from looking like a little old man to looking like a little kid on the first day of school. A little kid who thought Silly String was a good weapon. What next?

Ralph was sitting in the now infamous dugout, waiting.

"What took you guys so long? I could hear you talking ten minutes ago, but then you never came out of the woods."

"I was just showing Tracy my supplies." Lester took a seat beside Ralph. "Want to see?"

"That can wait," I said, giving Lester a do-not-open-that-bag-under-any-circumstances look. "We need to make a plan for the day. We have to find out who the money belongs to once and for all and how it came to be here."

I had my hands on my hips and was tapping my foot impatiently. We needed more information. It was like I could feel a clock hanging over my head, counting down the time before we had to hand in the money.

"I agree. I want this mystery over so things can be normal again," Ralph said.

I passed him the list I'd made the night before. He read it carefully, then sighed and passed it over to

Lester, who did the exact same thing. It irked me how well those two were getting along.

Ralph looked pained. "I thought it would be fun looking for clues, trying to find out who the money belonged to, but when it involves spying on people I like, I'm not so sure."

"You wish Joe Tunney wasn't on the list," I said.

"Yes," Ralph agreed, "because I'm positive he doesn't belong on it."

"Did you ever find him?" I asked. "It seems like he's gone from being everywhere to being nowhere. He didn't even deliver our newspaper this morning. Mom said that his younger sister did his route."

"That doesn't mean anything," Ralph said. "His sister's delivered his papers before."

"When he wasn't able to deliver them himself," I countered. "Do you know if he's sick or out of town?"

"No." Ralph's voice had a nasty edge to it, an edge he'd never used with me before. Suddenly, I wanted things to be normal again, too.

I crossed my arms over my chest and stared him

down. "I don't like your attitude. Do you want to work with Lester and me to solve this mystery or not?"

"Of course I do," Ralph said, but he still sounded touchy.

"Then don't be like that."

"Like what?"

Lester looked at Ralph and then up at me, shaking his head. "Get it together, Mr. and Mrs. Bickerson. Stop squabbling. One of our prime suspects just showed up."

That shut us up. I looked to where Lester was pointing. Joe Tunney was running the track again.

We watched Joe run three laps. None of us said a word.

Ralph finally broke the silence. "I guess we should go talk to him," he said. He sounded sad, and I almost said "let's forget it," but couldn't. In *The Maltese Falcon*, Humphrey Bogart had to question everyone, whether he wanted to or not. It was part of the job. Maybe we'd get lucky. Maybe Joe would have a valuable piece of information that would break the case wide open.

"Duh, you think?" I said. Ralph glared at me.

Lester looked between the two of us, disgusted.

"You two children can keep fighting if you like, but I'm going to talk to Joe to see if I can get him to confess to taking the money and hiding it here. Are you coming, Mr. and Mrs. Bickerson?"

I gave Lester a small shove forward and the three of us headed in Joe's direction. He'd done another complete loop, and by the time we reached the track he was stretching out his hamstrings.

I didn't know Joe well. He was two grades older than us, which meant he'd be going into his last grade of middle school come fall. Our conversations to date had mostly consisted of saying hello when he left the newspaper. He wasn't as tall as Ralph, but it was clear from watching him run that he was a natural athlete.

"Hi Joe," Ralph said. "I've been looking for you."

"Yeah?" Joe didn't sound like he wanted to be found. Ralph looked uncertain.

"We wanted to ask you about some missing money," I jumped in, giving Joe my million-dollar smile.

In return, I received a scowl. "You did, did you? Isn't that interesting? Maybe I want to talk to *you* about some missing money."

"I-I don't know what you mean," I stammered. *What did Joe know?*

He started to say something, but then stopped himself. When he spoke again, I could tell he was trying to sound calm and measured. "What missing money?"

I wasn't sure how to respond.

"Um—" I looked to Ralph for help.

And like a best friend, he jumped right in. "We heard that someone has either lost a lot of money or had a lot of money stolen."

Joe looked from Ralph to me, not blinking. "What would that have to do with me?"

"The money has a connection to the ball field," Lester said, sounding too cheerful. "So we need to talk to people who are here a lot. Like you."

It was as if Lester had slapped Joe. "Are you accusing me of stealing?" Joe demanded. "And whose money is it, anyway?"

Ralph and I exchanged a glance. "We're not sure," I finally said.

"It might belong to Hazel McNutt," Lester piped

up. I glared at him. This was too much information to share, especially when we weren't sure it was true.

"Why would I take money from Mrs. McNutt? I don't need to take anything. I earn it." He looked uncertain. "Did she ask you to ask me if I stole from her?" The hurt look on Joe's face would haunt me forever.

Our interrogation was unraveling. "Absolutely not. She has no idea we're asking you anything," I said.

"And we're not even sure she's missing money," Ralph added.

Joe's face had gone several shades of pink during our exchange, but now it had no color at all. "Let me get this straight: you guys found money. You don't know who it belongs to, you don't even know if it's stolen, and yet you're standing here asking me if I know anything about what could or could not be a crime, and you're accusing me of stealing it?" When he put it like that, it sounded awful. Ralph looked ready to throw up. Only Lester was keeping his composure.

"We're not asking if you stole it," Lester said, unzipping his knapsack and pulling out his notebook and a pen. "In fact, you might be the witness who can tell us who hid the paper bag in the dugout." Pen poised over paper, he waited for Joe to say something. When he didn't, Lester gave him a little prompt. "*Did* you see anybody leave a paper bag in the dugout sometime in the last few days?"

"I'm not answering any of your questions," Joe snapped. But then he seemed to think better of his response. "I've seen all kinds of activity around that dugout. I knew something weird was happening over there. And I know more than you think. For example, I saw you guys down on your hands and knees looking under one of the benches. For all I know, you're accusing me to divert attention away from *you*."

I gasped. He *had* seen us!

Joe gave me a triumphant smile. He was on the offensive now. He began to circle us, looking at each of us, sizing us up. "I saw other people hanging around that dugout, too."

"Who else did you see?" Ralph asked.

Joe shook his head. "You think I'd help you after you just accused me of being a thief? I wouldn't help you if you were the last people on Earth. How do I know *you're* not the thieves?"

"We didn't steal anything!" Ralph protested, taking a faltering step back. It was as though Joe had hit him.

"So you say . . ."

"How could we be the thieves?" I interrupted. "We're trying to figure out whose money it is and if it was stolen!"

"That's your story. Why should I believe you?" was Joe's bitter reply.

"To be fair, you've been following us around," Lester interjected. I felt grateful. It seemed to me that all logic had gone out of my head. "If you didn't have anything to do with the money, why follow us?"

Joe's grin was cold. "Maybe I was trying to figure out what you were up to. You guys looked pretty shady, creeping around town."

Ralph saw a glimmer of hope and grabbed for it. "We could work together to solve the case!"

"You don't have a case, Ralph. You're not a real detective. You're just a nosy kid. And I would never work with you."

Ralph looked devastated. Until that moment, I'd never realized how much Ralph looked up to Joe Tunney. Sure, he'd always talked about what a great guy Joe was, how he was a hard worker, how he never had a bad word to say about anyone, how he was always willing to help no matter how busy he was. The year Ralph had played hockey, Joe had spent extra time with him, helping him with his skating. He even loaned Ralph some of his hockey equipment, which was a big deal, because hockey equipment is expensive and Ralph's mom didn't have a lot of extra money for gear. Ralph said Joe was like a big brother because he always had his back. Since Ralph hadn't seen his father in years, I knew it was nice for him to have a guy to talk to about things now and then. I had the awful feeling that we had just wrecked their relationship forever.

"I've delivered the paper to your family for four years, Tracy." Joe's voice sounded on the verge of breaking and I could feel my eyes well up. "This is the thanks I get. And, Ralph, I thought we were friends. I feel like an idiot for ever being nice to you."

Joe's words cut deep. Why couldn't we have found

a better way to ask about the money? It occurred to me that if I were in Joe's shoes—if he was asking me the same questions—I would be just as upset.

"Joe, wait a second," Ralph was on the verge of tears. "Can't we talk some more? I know it sounds like we're accusing you, but we're not. We just want to figure out who the money belongs to. We got carried away. I'm sorry."

Before Joe could respond, his cell phone beeped. He looked down and cursed.

When he looked back up he shook his head. "Did you ever consider doing what normal people do when they find things that don't belong to them? Did you never think of just handing it in to the police and leaving it to them to find out whose money it was? Because, let me tell you something, you three are the worst detectives in the history of the world." Without sparing a glance for any of us, he turned and began to walk away. Then he broke into a run.

"I'm going after him," Ralph said. "I'll call you later."

Lester and I stood there, dumbfounded, as we watched Ralph pursue Joe across the track.

"That was awful," I finally said.

"That," Lester replied, "was the prime suspect telling us he's not the prime suspect."

"Do you think he was telling the truth?"

"I don't know him that well, but I don't believe he took the money. Tracy, what are we supposed to do now?"

I thought for a minute. Who knew how long Ralph would be gone? We needed to keep working. We needed to solve this case once and for all.

"Hazel's house," I said. "We need to go see Hazel."

CHAPTER 15

Instead of our usual route through the woods behind our house, we took the long way around so we could gather our thoughts. In the distance, I could see Jasmine walking a couple of blocks up the street. Even though I didn't want to ask her any questions, I thought I should. Jasmine was just the kind of person who would steal. Maybe I could trick her into confessing to the crime. If Jasmine had anything to do with the money, she was about to go from being our school's most popular troll to being a total nothing. Just the thought of that made me giddy. I elbowed Lester and pointed, and we jogged to catch up to her.

"Jasmine," I called as we got closer. "Wait up."

The perfectly tanned legs stopped moving and Jasmine whirled around. When she saw it was Lester and me, she put her hands on her hips as if we were the most exasperating individuals she had ever come across in her entire life.

"What do you want?" she asked. "I'm kind of in a hurry."

I swallowed my nasty response and kept my face emotionless. "I just wondered if you knew anything about misplaced money."

Her impatience was replaced by a look of concern. I couldn't decide if it was related to money being missing or if she was just worried that someone might think she was responsible.

"And I would talk about this with you, why?"

Jasmine had the uncanny ability of making me nervous. "I-I just know you've been over at the ball field a lot and that's where the money was found and I-I thought maybe you might have some ideas about how it came to be there." My face flushed with embarrassment.

"Again, I-I would tell you, why?" she mocked. "Because I think you're such an amazing person and

I'd want to help you solve another stupid mystery? Nuh-uh." She turned to go.

It was time to try a new tactic. I'd accuse her directly and make her confess, just like the detectives do in the movies. "I guess you and your friends are suspects. I mean, you've been hanging around the neighborhood a lot lately. You and the Ts were even seen hanging around the ball field. Maybe you stole the money from someone, like your aunt, and hid it over there."

Jasmine stepped forward and, for a second, I was sure she was going to hit me. Instead, she brought her face close to mine. "Listen to me, Tracy Munroe. I don't know anything about any money. Until you mentioned it a minute ago, I'd never heard about money being lost or stolen. And I don't know why you're mentioning my Aunt Hazel. She's never said anything to me about missing any money. If I were you, I'd be careful with your accusations. If you repeat what you just said to me or to anybody else, I'll have my mom call our lawyer!"

I gulped.

"Maybe you didn't take money and hide it there,

but that doesn't mean one of your friends didn't do it," Lester jumped in. His words gave me courage.

"He's right," I said. "Maybe one of the Ts did it."

Jasmine's eyes narrowed into two slits. "I know how you work. You're accusing me and my friends because you're jealous of me. Why should I even believe you? Maybe I should call the police and let them sort it out. Because it sounds to me like you found money that doesn't belong to you and you haven't turned it in." She spotted the look of panic on my face and smirked. "Ha, I was right! There's only one unfortunate thing."

"What's that?" Lester asked. He hadn't yet grasped that Jasmine had turned the tables on us.

She sneered at him. "That because she's a kid, they probably won't lock your sister up and throw away the key. I would love to see your sister go to jail." With that, she flounced off, leaving a stunned Lester and me in her wake.

"That went well," Lester said. "I hope things go better at Hazel's."

"She's going to rat us out," I moaned.

"Then we have to go see Hazel right now. If it isn't her money, we need to get the package and take it to the police right away."

I gave him a miserable nod. I hated to admit it, but he was right. Our time had run out.

There was a strange car in Hazel's driveway, a metallic silver convertible with a cream leather interior. It was the nicest car I'd ever seen. I glanced into the backseat and saw a brown leather briefcase and all kinds of over-sized, rolled-up papers.

"I wonder who's visiting Hazel?" I said to Lester.

Lester looked at me as if I had four heads. "That's Zach's dad's car. Haven't you noticed it in the driveway since we've been back?"

I shook my head. "I don't think so. I haven't met Zach's dad yet. Have you?"

Lester nodded. "The Silver Fox."

"The Silver Fox?" I said. "What's that mean?"

Lester grinned. "Don't you remember? That's what Hazel called him in the caption of the picture we saw of the two of them on Facebook."

I'd forgotten all about that Facebook picture.

"Look, here's your chance to meet him. He's coming out."

We stood in the driveway, looking like a couple of valet drivers waiting to give someone their car at a fancy hotel.

"Hi, Mr. Favola," Lester called, as an older man came toward us carrying a silver travel mug and another briefcase. Hazel was hot on his heels.

"Hello yourself, Mr. Munroe," Mr. Favola said. I looked at Lester in wonder. He knew everyone. I thought I was the person with her finger on the pulse of the neighborhood, but it seemed I was an amateur compared to my brother. "And this must be the lovely Tracy I have been hearing so much about."

I was sure that the blush started in my big toes and climbed the whole length of my body, rendering each successive part completely unable to function like a normal human being. I knew I should say hello, but all

I could do was stare at the wonder that was Mr. Favola. Unlike Zach, his dad had a bit of an Italian accent, which only made him more exotic to me. He was wearing a light gray suit and a shiny mint-green tie, and was the most elegant person I'd ever seen. Even though Mr. Favola was old—he looked about Hazel's age, which put him in his early fifties—and had a head of curly silver hair, I could understand why Hazel liked him. And I could see where Zach got his good looks. Mr. Favola was, to quote Jasmine and her pals, a total hottie.

Luckily Hazel was there to help me out of my stupefied state. "Hello, Tracy. What are you and Lester up to today?"

"We came by to see Zach," I said. Lester looked at me, confused. I was suddenly afraid to talk to Hazel. What if she got mad? What if Mr. Favola wanted to be a part of the conversation, too, and then told Zach? I'd made such a big deal out of the mystery to impress Zach. I didn't want him to realize how badly I'd botched the whole thing.

"He's working right now," Mr. Favola said. "Would you like me to take you to see him? I'm on my way to the construction site anyway, so it wouldn't be any inconvenience."

"Um, sure," I said. I knew I should go clear things up with Hazel. But now that she was standing right in front of me, the thought of talking to her made me want to throw up. Maybe Zach had remembered something that would help me solve the case. If he hadn't, what difference could an hour make anyway?

I leaned over and whispered in Lester's ear, "I'm going to visit Zach, ask if he's seen anything suspicious, and come right back, okay? That way we'll have interviewed everybody before we talk to Hazel."

"You already talked to Zach," Lester pointed out. Darn his memory!

"Yeah, but maybe he knows something new. Maybe he took the money. I'll try and trick him—"

Lester cut me off. "Like you tricked Jasmine? Don't go. We need to talk to Hazel right away and see if the money is hers. And you can't fool me. I know all about you and Zach."

I froze, and then took a deep breath to make sure I sounded relaxed. "What do you mean?"

Lester whispered back, "I saw you with him last night. I heard you talking, and I know you're working with him. Ralph's going to be so mad."

I leaned in, my face so close to my brother's that our noses were practically touching. "You said you wouldn't eavesdrop again! Anyway, it isn't what you think. It's—"

"I know exactly what it is. Fine—go tell Zach you're not working with him anymore. You're only working with us, okay? If not, I'm going to tell Ralph."

"You're blackmailing me!"

"You should have thought of that before you decided to be in cahoots with the enemy." For a nine-year-old brat, Lester sure had a big vocabulary.

"Fine, I'll tell Zach he's off the case. Just keep your mouth shut, Pig Face. Wait here and keep an eye on things. As soon as I get back, I promise we'll talk to Hazel."

I couldn't believe my plans had been tripped up by Lester's snooping and my own stupidity. Of course he would be skulking around, watching me; he was *always* skulking around. Plus, I should have known it would be impossible to work with Lester. He couldn't be trusted. I couldn't wait for the case to be over so I could kick him back to the curb. Could this day get any worse?

He grinned wickedly at me. "The name's Lester. Don't be too long, okay? And keep your walkie-talkie on." I didn't bother to tell him that the walkie-talkie only worked within a one-block radius. Let him figure that out himself.

Meanwhile, Mr. Favola was still chatting with Hazel beside the car. "Don't forget about our dinner plans tonight, pretty lady."

Hazel beamed. The effect was startling. I hadn't seen her look happy in such a long time that I'd forgotten that she could look pretty. "I'll be ready, Silver Fox." If I hadn't been so stressed, I would have gagged. She and Mr. Favola were acting like a couple of lovesick teenagers.

"Hop in!" Mr. Favola said turning to me, and I opened the door and stepped into the most glamorous car ever. I pulled my red, heart-shaped sunglasses out of my purse and put them on, feeling like an old-time movie star, like a girl who should be riding around in a convertible. The painful memories of my conversations with Joe and Jasmine, and of being busted by Lester, were forgotten in the excitement of getting to pretend I was Grace Kelly, driving with Cary Grant in the movie *To Catch a Thief*.

"Thanks for the drive," I said, trying to strike up a conversation. I wanted Mr. Favola to like me, to think I was worthy of being Zach's friend. As we drove along, I kept hoping that everyone I knew would see me riding around town in a convertible. I especially hoped to see Jasmine and the Ts. I knew they would die of jealousy if they saw me with Zach's father.

"No trouble at all," he said. "I know Zach's been a bit lonely since he got here, what with me working all the time and his mother and friends so far away. I was glad when he mentioned how nice he thought you were."

I imagined Zach and his dad eating an exotic meal while watching a foreign film, casually discussing how wonderful I was. They were so different from everyone else in town. If Zach was talking to his dad about me, it meant he liked me. I wondered if he'd told his mom about me yet. I bet he told her how much I loved musicals. She'd think I was the perfect friend for him and invite me to visit them in New York City.

The longer we drove, the happier I felt. My worries about Hazel and Jasmine floated away. Everything would be fine. We went a few blocks, and then turned down onto a cul-de-sac, parking in front of a big Victorian house that looked like it belonged on a Hallmark card. I knew the house well—it belonged to our school librarian, Mrs. Smythe.

"Zach's working here?" I asked. I noticed signs of fresh paint on the front porch steps.

Mr. Favola got out of the car and inspected the steps. When he climbed back in he muttered "sloppy" and pulled out his phone. "He must have gone to his next job. Let me check his schedule."

He slid through several screens until he found what he was looking for. Holding it toward me, he showed me a calendar with several names written on it.

"Okay, he's either mowing the Nicholsons' lawn or at the Garcelons' trimming a hedge. Oh wait. He could be out on the Ledge Road, too. He's supposed to paint a shed at some place called the Cogswell Farm. We're lucky Hazel found him so many jobs."

"Wow, he's really busy," I said, studying the calendar in Mr. Favola's hand. I wondered if Zach was grateful that Hazel had found him so many chores.

"Zach's the kind of boy who needs to keep busy or he gets into trouble. His mother and I thought a summer in a small town would do him good. St. Stephen is such a pretty place. It reminds me of the small town where I grew up. In New York City, there are a lot of opportunities to get into trouble. Plus, I'm sure his mother needed a break from him."

His mother needed a break from him? What kind of thing was that to say about your son?

Zach didn't seem like trouble to me. "He seems to be working hard," I offered.

Mr. Favola laughed, and not in a kind way. "He works only as much as he's forced to."

I decided to change the subject. "It must be nice to spend the summer together. Do you get to see each other a lot when you're in New York City?" As soon as the question popped out of my mouth, I wished I could pull it back in. It was none of my business.

Mr. Favola shrugged. "It's nice to spend the summer with him, but I wish he had a better attitude about it." He turned to me and smiled. "Perhaps now that he's hanging out with a nice girl like you, he'll cultivate a better perspective on life." I had no idea what Mr. Favola was talking about, but I nodded anyway.

"This is a great car. I've never driven in such a nice one before."

Mr. Favola beamed. "I worked hard to get this car," he said, stroking the dashboard like it was his favorite pet. "My father worked hard, too. He held down two jobs to keep our family going. One of them was as a train conductor, so I didn't get to spend much time with him. I didn't mind. My job was to take care of my mother and my younger brother. Kids today have it too easy."

I wanted to protest on behalf of all kids, but I didn't want to get on Mr. Favola's bad side. The story of his childhood reminded me of Ralph. Ralph's dad had left his mom about five years ago and moved out west. Ralph never complains about it, though. He just helps his Mom and Willie and does what needs doing. I swallowed hard. I needed to apologize to Ralph as soon as possible.

Mr. Favola was still talking. He seemed to enjoy hearing himself speak. "If I can give you a piece of advice about money, here it is: you've got to keep your money safe. Hide it from the tax man. Oh, and one more thing: you'd be amazed how much money you can get just by keeping your eyes open for opportunity. And when you see that money—BAM!—you grab it!"

If I hadn't already been seated, I would have fallen over. Mr. Favola sounded like somebody who wouldn't feel guilty about stealing! Could he have taken the money?

"I say that to Zach all the time. But does he ever listen? No, he does not. He's a spender, not a saver. And he needs the money. He wants to go to Italy with me at Christmas. I have relatives there he hasn't seen since he was a little boy. I told him to save lots of money so he can go, too. If not—ciao baby—I'll go alone."

I glanced at the fancy car, the beautiful suit, the expensive sunglasses, and couldn't help wondering why

Mr. Favola wouldn't just buy Zach's ticket instead of making him work at all those jobs. I guessed he wanted to build Zach's character. My parents were always trying to build mine, and their tactics almost always involved babysitting Lester or cleaning.

"Let's try the Nicholson house first, shall we?" Mr. Favola said. I nodded, but it didn't matter because he spun the car around quickly and we were off, tearing through town again. I hoped that Zach wasn't working out at Ledge Road. That was at least a mile walk from my house and it would take me a lot longer to get back to Lester. My brother on his own was a dangerous thing. What if he told Ralph everything? What if he talked to Hazel by himself? My decision to put off talking to her was seeming more foolish by the minute.

As we approached the Nicholsons', I released a giant sigh of relief. There was Zach, mowing the side lawn. He didn't see us at first. When he finally did, he began to walk toward the convertible. It was hard to tell if he was pleased or peeved that his dad had brought me along.

"Here she is, sport!" Mr. Favola's voice was cheerful,

but it was a fake kind of cheerful and it made me nervous. I hopped out of the car.

Zach looked from me to his father. "Give me a second, okay?" he said, directing me toward the lawn mower. As I walked away, I caught a word here and there, each one more upsetting than the last: "Wrong girl"; "What were you thinking?"; and, worst of all, "Jasmine." I couldn't help turning around when I heard her name. From the look of horror on Mr. Favola's face, it was clear to me that the girl Zach had been talking up to his dad was my archenemy, not me. I stood frozen in place, stupidly waiting for this boy who wished I wasn't there. How had I been so wrong?

As they continued their conversation, Mr. Favola suddenly pointed to a part of the lawn that Zach had just finished mowing.

"You're going to have to do that over again," he said. "There's no way I would pay someone who did such a lousy job on *my* lawn."

"You don't even have a house," Zach said.

That seemed to set Mr. Favola off. He hopped out

of the car and began to walk the yard, cursing when the freshly mown grass stained his fancy shoes.

"Look!" he shouted. "I see uneven patches there, there, and for sure over there. I want you to redo this whole mess before these Nicholson people see the sloppy job you've done and call me to complain."

"They're nice people. They won't complain," was Zach's sullen reply.

"Then they're idiots, boy," Mr. Favola spat back. Meanwhile, I continued to stand off to the side, mortified to be there, and embarrassed for Zach that his father was treating him so poorly in front of me.

Finally, Mr. Favola started losing steam. "We'll talk more about this tonight," he said as he climbed back into his car, careful to avoid touching the creamy leather with his green-tinged shoes.

"Whatever," Zach said.

"Whatever is right, young man," Mr. Favola said, and then backed out of the driveway, driving away at a speed much higher than the posted limit.

Zach stood with his back to me for a good three or four minutes, not speaking.

"I'm sorry I let your dad bring me over," I called out finally. "I guess he thought I was Jasmine."

When Zach turned, I could tell he was on the verge of crying.

"You see how mean he is, right?"

His father was terrible, but I didn't think it was polite to say so, so I didn't reply.

Anxious to change the topic and get back to Lester, I plowed on. "I just popped over to tell you that we still don't know who the thief is. We're going to go see Hazel in a few minutes and tell her that we found money and ask if it's hers."

Zach said nothing.

"Your dad will cool down, you know," I added, gesturing toward the mowed lawn that looked perfectly fine to me.

Half-smiling, half-crying, Zach shook his head. "Nah, nothing's ever good enough for him. Anyway, it doesn't matter. I'll be going home to my mom soon enough. I can't wait. If I could, I'd get on a bus tonight."

"Maybe you could call your mom?"

"No, it just makes her upset when I talk to her about dad. I'll just have to wait it out, unless it gets even worse." He stood quietly for a moment, looking sad and thoughtful. Then the clouds seemed to pass and he brought his attention back to me. "Are you going to take Hazel the money when you talk to her?"

"No. We don't know for sure that it's hers. We'll talk to her and if she confirms our suspicions, we'll go get the money. If not, we're going to take it to the police."

"I hope you hid the cash somewhere safe. Is it at your house or Ralph's?"

"Neither. We decided to hide it at this place in the woods where we hang out sometimes."

Zach peered down at his watch. "That's good. Look, I gotta get back to work. I need to be over at the Garcelons' house soon. See you later?"

Not waiting for a response, he popped his earbuds in, turned on his iPod, and got back to work, as if I wasn't there at all.

As I watched him mow a couple of rows, I felt so sorry for him that I wanted to cry. Even though it hurt that Zach liked Jasmine better than me, I still liked him. I wanted his dad to treat him better. Maybe Hazel would be willing to talk to Mr. Favola and make him understand that the way he was treating Zach hurt his feelings. I'd ask her when Lester and I went to see her.

Ugh. Thinking of going to see Hazel made the awful feeling in my stomach return. But I'd avoided the meeting long enough.

My phone buzzed: Ralph. **At the ball field. We need to talk.** Had Lester ratted me out? If he had, my day was about to go from horrible to the worst one ever.

Chapter 16

Ralph was waiting for me in the dugout holding his head in his hands.

"This is like déjà vu all over again," I joked, plunking myself down beside him.

Normally, when I said something like that, Ralph would give me a funny response. Not this time. When he turned his head toward me, he looked like the world was ending.

"It didn't go well with Joe, huh?" I asked. Ralph winced like I'd slapped him.

"He wouldn't talk to me," Ralph said. He reached down and began picking at the side of his Chucks where a big hole was forming near his big toe. Ralph's feet seemed like they would never stop growing and, for some reason, I couldn't help but wonder if all that growing hurt.

Watching him pick at his shoes made me nervous. I began to chew on another cuticle. "We handled our talk with him badly. He wouldn't talk to you at all?"

Ralph's mouth twisted into a grimace. "When I tried, the only thing he said was that he would never have believed that I was like everyone else. He thought I was better than that."

"Ouch."

Ralph looked at me and nodded. "*Ouch* is right. I *am* better than this, Tracy. How have we made such a mess of everything?"

"I don't know. But I don't think we're very good detectives."

The questions tumbled out of his mouth. "Did you talk to Hazel? Was the money hers? Do you think she'll accuse Joe of taking it?"

"Lester and I haven't gone to see her yet. We ran into Jasmine and asked her what she knew, but it was clear that if Hazel's missing money, she never told Jasmine."

"Another thing we got wrong," was Ralph's depressed reply.

"Jasmine didn't seem to know anything useful, although she did say if anyone was missing money it was probably us that took it. And she hopes I end up in jail."

"She said that? We have to turn that money in today. I can't do this anymore. What if Jasmine goes to the police?"

"She won't do that, Ralph. We'll march over to Hazel's right now."

Ralph jumped up and began to frantically pace the dugout, his hands holding his temples. "What if Hazel thinks we took her money, even when we give it back? What if she's always suspicious of us going forward? What if we've cost Joe his job? He relies on that money, you know."

"Calm down. We'll deal with that when it happens. First things first. And face it: if Hazel's going to be mad at anyone, it's me."

Ralph stopped and looked at me. "You're right. Your parents are going to kill you."

Maybe we'd catch a lucky break and the money wasn't Hazel's after all. Maybe we could still be heroes.

"Let's get this over with. Sitting here isn't helping anyone. But we need to stick together, okay?"

Neither of us said anything for a while. I couldn't take the tension. "Where's Lester?"

"Last time I saw him he was with you."

With so much going on, I was losing my ability to keep track of all the moving pieces. "Oh, right. I left him at Hazel's when I went for the drive with Mr. Favola." My heart sunk a little as I remembered how that had turned out. Lester was going to be annoyed that I hadn't come straight back.

"Why'd you go for a drive with Mr. Favola?" Ralph's tone was suspicious.

I tried to make my response as light as possible. "I don't know. I always wanted to drive in a convertible, I guess. He was going to work so he dropped me off where Zach was mowing a lawn."

"Figures," Ralph said. "You leave all the dirty work to me and Lester while you go and gallivant around town."

I turned toward Hazel's house. "I'm not even

justifying that remark with a response, Ralph Huffman. And I was not gallivanting around town. I was doing detective work. C'mon, let's go talk to Hazel. Then we'll find Lester and the three of us can go to the Big Rock for the money so we can put an end to this whole stupid mystery."

P P P

A teary but smiling Hazel opened her front door. I'd expected to find Lester there with her, since there was no sign of him in the backyard, but she was alone.

"I'm glad you're here—" she began, but I cut her off.

"We need to talk to you about some money we found," I said, trying hard to look her in the eye when all I wanted to do was crawl under a nearby table.

"Isn't that funny? That's what I wanted to talk to the two of you about," she said, ushering us inside.

We followed her into the living room. It was the first time I'd been in her house. Ralph had described it, but he hadn't fully prepared me for her decorating scheme. Like Hazel, it was over the top. Fortunately, my fear of what Hazel would say when we told her the truth erased all of the usual wisecracks right out of my head. I took a seat on the brilliant purple couch while Ralph eased onto one of the pink velvet side chairs. Hazel took the other, the one that was paired with a bright orange ottoman. We sat quietly for a moment. My eyes darted from the coffee table with the mirrored top upon which Hazel had placed a naked cherub, to the lime green walls, and then to the huge black and white photograph of Hazel holding an antique doll. It was a scary sight: the lips of both Hazel and the doll had been tinted a deep blood red. I began to feel dizzy.

Hazel cleared her throat. "Joe Tunney was just here, and a very startling thing happened."

I looked over at Ralph. "What kind of a startling thing?" I croaked. My voice felt like it was being stolen, probably by the scary cherub in front of me.

"Joe heard I might have had some money stolen and he wanted to talk to me, make sure I knew that he hadn't taken it . . ." Her voice trailed off and she pulled a Kleenex out of the sleeve of her sweater and dabbed at her eyes.

"Before I could say anything, he started asking *me* questions." She smiled at us. "Do you know how smart he is? When he grows up, he's planning on going to college so he can study to be an astrophysicist. Can you imagine that, a boy from St. Stephen becoming an astrophysicist? Of course if anybody can, it would be Joe."

"*Have* you had any money stolen?" I asked, dreading the answer.

"I thought so, yes. When you asked me the other day if I knew if anyone was missing any money, Tracy, it reminded me that I'd forgotten to deposit some money that I'd been carrying in my purse. The money you got out of the attic for me, Ralph."

"I didn't get any money out of the attic for you!" Ralph protested.

Hazel laughed. "Oh that's right—I didn't tell you what was inside that box I asked you to fetch down for me."

"You keep money in boxes?" I asked. Was there *nothing* normal about Hazel McNutt?

Hazel laughed. "Not typically. I remembered that

Mr. McNutt had been saving American money for a trip we were planning to take to Florida. Anytime someone gave him an American bill, he'd throw it in a box he kept on the shelf in the closet. I guess he forgot it when he moved out. Anyway, after a couple of months, I packed everything he'd left behind and threw it all up into the attic, including the box with the money in it. It was only a few weeks ago that I even remembered the box. I wasn't sure there was money in it—that's why I wanted you to go up and get it for me, Ralph. Imagine my surprise when I saw the box had nearly two thousand dollars in it."

"We found American money over in the dugout at the ball field," I confessed, keeping my eyes firmly fixed on my hands so I wouldn't see the rage I knew was coming. "But there wasn't that much money in the bag."

"Ah," was all Hazel said. The room was quiet for a minute.

"What kind of questions did Joe ask you?" Ralph had finally found his voice.

"He asked if I was certain that the money was stolen.

You know, could I have misplaced it, dropped it some-where, that sort of thing."

"And?"

"To be honest, I wasn't sure, but then Joe helped me remember the day I'd lost the bag. He talked me through the whole day, from breakfast till bedtime: what I did, and where I went, and who I was with."

My knee was starting to jiggle in anticipation. "And?" I prompted.

"We walked through every hour. And while we were sitting there, Joe said, 'Mrs. McNutt, do you know your purse is unzipped?' and I said, 'Oh yes, it's always unzipped' and then Joe looked at me and I looked at him and I think we both came to the same conclusion: that maybe the money wasn't stolen at all."

Ralph looked at me, a look of total confusion on his face.

"What do you mean?" I asked. I was feeling con-fused, too.

"I always wander around town with my purse unzipped. It's a terrible, silly habit. Things fall out all the time, although they mostly fall out in the car. And while Joe and I talked, it became crystal clear: I probably lost the money when I was sitting in the dugout with John."

"You were sitting in the dugout with Mr. Favola?" I said. Ralph looked at me. We remembered the picture of the two of them on Facebook. We would have solved the case a lot sooner if we'd known they were sitting in the dugout.

"Yes, we had gone for a walk and ended up over by the ball field. It was a warm evening and we decided to sit in the dugout for a few minutes, take a little break before we walked back home. I'm sure I lost it there. I'd set my purse on the ground near my feet, and when I went to pick it up, I kicked it by mistake and a bunch of things flew out scattering underneath the bench: my lipstick, a makeup bag, a romance novel that I always carry with me, my Tic Tacs. Of course the bag of money must have fallen out, too, but I forgot it had been in my bag, and it was dark by then. I guess John and I missed it when we were picking everything else up."

"But why were you carrying around that much

money in a paper bag?" I asked. "When we found the money, we were sure it was stolen because of the bag."

"I couldn't find an envelope, so I threw it in a small paper bag instead. I didn't think it was a big deal. I was planning to go to the bank the next morning to deposit it."

"Huh," I said. I didn't know what else to say. I'd been so sure the money had been hidden in the dugout by a thief. Who carried money in a paper bag? And if I was being honest, I wanted it to be a thief. This was just like Principal Walton's Cadillac all over again. I felt so stupid. It also explained why everyone seemed so innocent when we talked to them; they *were* innocent.

"Huh, is right," Hazel agreed. "Of course, I apologized to Joe profusely for even suspecting him, and he was gracious enough to accept my apology. I wanted to go to the dugout and look for it, but Joe said it wasn't there."

"He said that?" Ralph whispered.

"Yes, but he said he was sure it would come back to me today. And now I guess I know why he was so sure. Somebody *did* find it."

Somebody found it and made a mystery out of it, I thought. Joe figured out that Ralph and Lester and I had the money. I couldn't believe he hadn't told Hazel. *He must be giving us a chance to do the right thing.*

"I feel so relieved," she continued. "It wasn't a large sum, so if it was gone, it wasn't going to ruin me or anything. But I felt bad, because I began to suspect all kinds of people of taking the money: Joe, Zach, Jasmine. Even you, Ralph."

Ralph looked sick. "We didn't take your money, Mrs. McNutt—we found it."

Hazel smiled and held out her hand. "I know you didn't take it. If you'll just hand it over, I can run down to the bank right away and finally get it deposited where it will be safe and sound."

"We don't have it," I whispered.

The kind look on Hazel's face began to morph into her regular grouchy mask. "Oh no—don't tell me you lost my money!"

Ralph shook his head. "Oh no. We've hidden it someplace safe. We can go get it right now. We didn't want to bring it until we knew it was yours. We'd planned to take it to the police if it wasn't."

Hazel relaxed. "Phew. But I don't understand why you've had the money these past days and haven't turned it in."

I slumped down so far that I was practically sliding onto the floor. "It's my fault. I wanted to try and solve a mystery. But I wasn't a very good detective. . . ."

Hazel gave me a funny look. She started to say something, but then stopped herself. After a couple of minutes of silence she finally spoke. "Why don't you kids run and get the money. When you come back, we can have some milk and cookies and talk."

Hazel McNutt was inviting us for milk and cookies? I stared at her, my mouth hanging open. Fortunately, Ralph had more sense than I did. "That would be great Mrs. McNutt."

He stood up, motioned for me to do the same, and we stumbled and mumbled our way out of the house.

Outside, the once clear sky was being attacked by dark rain clouds.

"Can you believe the money wasn't stolen?" I asked, as we cut through the hedge to my yard.

Ralph shook his head. He looked sick. "You're wrong."

"What do you mean?"

"The money *was* stolen. We stole it."

CHAPTER 17

"This is bad," Ralph moaned. "My mom is going to kill me when she finds out about this. I'll be grounded forever."

"Yeah, me too," I said. "Only my punishment will be even worse because my parents will accuse me of dragging Pig Face into this with us."

"Ha! Pig Face was a willing accomplice."

"Willing accomplice? Now you're talking like a crook!"

"Well? Isn't that what we are? Crooks?"

I reached for the doorknob and put my finger in front of my mouth. "Shhhh. We can talk about our life in prison after we grab Lester and get the money.

We'll make a plan. Everything will be fine." I sounded a lot more certain than I felt. In my mind, I was already picking out which stuffed animal to take with me to jail and trying to figure out if I'd be allowed to bedazzle the jumpsuit they'd make me wear.

Ralph and I walked inside, quiet as monks. My house was equally silent. It felt like the calm before a great big storm. I checked every room. No Lester.

Mom had left a note on the kitchen table that said *Gone for groceries.* I picked it up and held the paper out for Ralph to see. "Lester never misses a chance to go to the grocery store. You know how he loves his cereal. Let's go to the Big Rock ourselves and get the money. He won't care. By the time we get back, he'll be here and he can come over to Hazel's with us. Maybe she'll go easy on us if he's there. A lot of grown-ups think he's cute."

Our walk to the Big Rock was more like a funeral march. Neither Ralph nor I really wanted to talk. We were both lost in our own thoughts. I was imagining the untold eternal punishments that awaited us when we took the money back to Hazel, because for sure she would tell our moms what we had done. It was going to be ugly. A lot uglier than the time Ralph and I left school at recess on the first day of kindergarten because we were bored and felt we'd learned enough.

And then there was Jasmine. She would definitely find out what we'd done and, anyway, Lester and I had kind of given things away during our botched attempt to interrogate her. I was sure I'd never live down Lester's lisp, but that was nothing compared to Ralph and me taking the money and trying to solve a mystery like Hollywood ace detectives.

We stopped at the base of the Big Rock. Ralph waited while I crouched down, pushed the curtain of branches aside, and reached in for the bag. I couldn't feel it at first, so I felt around inside the crevice. Nothing.

"The bag's not there," I said, my hand moving frantically now. I even ignored the creepy things I was touching in my quest to find that stupid bag.

"What do you mean, the bag's not there?" Ralph gasped. I stepped aside and he reached into the crevice himself. Then he moved to the ground nearby and searched under some other bushes. When that failed, he climbed, panting, up to the top of the Big Rock and looked everywhere. I followed behind him, a sense of dread overtaking me. I could barely breathe.

I expected Ralph to freak out, but he stayed calm. After assuring himself the bag was definitely gone, he said, "Lester's been here. That's the only reasonable explanation. I don't know why Lester would have taken the money, but I'm sure he's keeping it safe. Besides, he's the only other person who knows we hid it here." As Ralph finished his sentence, I noticed a black candy bar wrapper on the ground nearby. I picked it up: Dylan's Candy Bar. I sucked in my breath and held it out for Ralph to see.

"What's that?"

"One of Zach's candy bar wrappers." But how could Zach have found the Big Rock? And why would he take the money?

Ralph stared down at me. As he read my face, his calm demeanor was replaced, second-by-second, by a cold, bitter rage.

"Ralph—" I started.

"You told him, didn't you? You told that idiot where we hid the money."

"No, I didn't, I swear—"

"There's no other way he could find this place. You told him about our sacred hideout."

I held up a hand. "Wait! Don't you remember the first time we brought Lester out here—I was sure I saw someone in the bushes near the railway tracks on our way here. I bet it was Zach. He must have followed us and seen our hiding spot."

"It's pretty convenient that only you saw him." Ralph's voice was like ice.

My eyes welled up. I didn't want to cry, but the look of disgust on Ralph's face made me feel small and desperate. Ralph had never accused me of lying before.

I thought back to the many lies I had told over the past few days. They were all catching up with me. My voice quavered. "I'm telling you the truth. I have no idea how Zach found the money. It doesn't make any sense. I thought he was working with us, and . . ." I gulped, wishing I could pluck my last words out of the air and put them back in my mouth.

Ralph sneered at the single tear that was now making its way down my cheek. "I knew you were doing something with that creep! I knew it! And I don't need you to tell me why you told him about our secret hideout and the money. You thought it would make him like you more than he likes Jasmine. Ha! Like that would ever happen."

"I didn't tell him about the Big Rock! And as for working with him, yes, I admit I told him about the money to impress him. So what? He wanted to help."

"Help himself to Hazel's money."

I couldn't argue. "I wouldn't have had to work with him in secret if you'd only tried to like him. I don't know why you think he's such a bad guy, anyway. What's he ever done to you? You hardly even know him."

"Trust me. He *is* a bad guy."

Something snapped inside me. "So you say. But I'm not the only one keeping secrets—you've been keeping something from me ever since I came back from vacation."

"What do you mean?"

"Why won't you tell me what you've been doing for Hazel McNutt?"

Embarrassment rolled across Ralph's face. "I told you. She asked me not to tell anyone, and when I give my word—unlike other people—I keep it."

"Well that's mighty convenient. Why should I believe you?"

Ralph threw his hands up in the air. "Fine, you want to know the truth? Here it is: I've been giving Hazel cooking lessons so she can impress Zach's dad. Happy now?"

"You've been giving Hazel McNutt cooking lessons?"

"Yeah, I needed the money. Willie's birthday is in a couple of weeks and Mom and I really want to buy him a new gaming system, but it's expensive. Now you know my *deep, dark* secret. I wonder how long until you blab it all over the neighborhood."

"I won't blab it. But I wish you'd told me before. I felt like I couldn't trust you anymore."

Ralph raised his eyes skyward. When he focused on me again, he seemed different. He didn't look like my best friend anymore. He was glaring at me like Jasmine had earlier in the day, like he couldn't stand the sight of me. "You know what? I don't care if you trust me now or not, Tracy Munroe, because I sure don't trust you. And you know why I don't like Zach? Because every single time I was over at Hazel's he made fun of me—of my height, my love of cooking, everything about me. And I couldn't say anything back because I was working for Hazel and I needed the money and I knew she liked Zach. Or, at least, she likes his dad, which is kind of the same thing. He thinks he's so cool because he's from New York City, but all he is is someone who tears down other people so he can feel better about himself. And he may not have stolen Hazel's money to begin with, but he sure has now. That means that you're friends with a thief. I hope you'll be very happy together."

I leaned away, feeling the words Ralph was raining down on me were like blows. "I'm so sorry. I didn't realize it was that bad."

Ralph laughed as if what I'd said was the funniest thing he'd ever heard. "Yeah, you didn't know. So what? You trusted him more than me. Me—your best friend. Do you know how that makes me feel? If you told me you didn't like someone, I'd take that seriously, even if you didn't feel like you wanted to share your reasons why with me. And you know why? Because we're friends, and that's what friends do. Now look where we are because of you. First we took Hazel's money, and now we've lost it."

"I can make this right."

Ralph shook his head. "How, Tracy? It'll be our word against his. And I bet he's hidden the bag somewhere we'll never find it. If you go back and tell Hazel that Zach's taken her money, you think she'll believe us? She doesn't even like us, Tracy! And even if she does believe us, we'll probably wreck her relationship with Mr. Favola. We didn't take care of her money."

Ralph's voice was getting louder and louder and I shrunk back against the onslaught of words.

"And yeah, maybe you can make it right with Hazel, Tracy, but you can never make it right with me. I thought we were a team. I thought we were best friends!"

I felt woozy. Everything was wrong. "It was a mistake, Ralph! Come on. I was just talking too much, like I always do. We *are* best friends!" The tears were flowing for real now, and I didn't even try to brush them away.

"Best friends don't lie to each other. You betrayed me. You betrayed your own brother. Do you remember that day in the barn, Tracy, the day you told Lester that the bag of money was a mystery?"

I nodded.

"The only mystery is how someone as smart as you could be so stupid. How you could throw everything away to make some creep think you're cool and to get back at Jasmine. As far as I'm concerned, we're not friends anymore. I'm done with you. You fix things with Hazel. I'm going home." As Ralph brushed by me to climb down from the rock, I could see that his face was crumpling like mine, and I knew it had taken every ounce of strength he had not to cry in front of me.

"Ralph!" I called after him. "I can fix this!"

But the only response was the sound of twigs snapping as Ralph ran as fast as he could to get away from me.

CHAPTER 18

I stumbled and tripped my way home, crying and desperately hoping that Lester was back. I had to find Zach and try and get back the money, but I wanted Lester with me for support. I couldn't face Zach alone.

The house was still empty, which made me even more upset. I needed to talk to Lester. He would be angry with me, but he wouldn't stay mad. I wasn't sure I could say the same about Ralph. *Lester and Mom probably stopped somewhere for a snack*, I thought, and then realized I hadn't eaten a thing since breakfast. I grabbed a couple of crackers, needing all the strength I could get.

Doh! Doh! Doh! The Homer Simpson clock struck

three. Three o'clock. Six hours since Lester and I'd gone to meet Ralph. It felt like a lifetime ago. As I nibbled the crackers, I replayed my conversation with Ralph over and over again. Every look he'd given me felt like a stab to my heart now. How had I been so stupid? How had I let my anger at Jasmine and my fascination with Zach wreck the only true friendship I had?

At the end of *The Maltese Falcon*, Humphrey Bogart sends Mary Astor off to jail. Trixie had warned me that I was choosing the tragic couple. How had I forgotten that? The Sam Spade character might love her, but he wasn't fooled by her, just like Ralph wasn't fooled by me. What would I do without Ralph? I might find other friends someday, but they would never be Ralph. The rest of the summer and sixth grade stretched ahead of me, bleak and lonely. I wondered if Mom would let me go to boarding school.

After another bite of a tear-soaked cracker, I decided I'd avoided my responsibilities long enough. I needed to find Zach. Now. I tried to remember where he was working. My best guess was that he was still at the Garcelons' house, trimming their hedge. Hedge trimming took time, especially ones that large. I wiped my eyes. Confronting Zach was never going to get any easier.

♀ ♀ ♀

When I arrived at the Garcelons', I knew I'd made a mistake. Zach was holding court with Jasmine and the Ts. The four girls were lying on the grass all around him, their T-shirts knotted just below the bras they didn't need. I looked down at the outfit I'd been so proud of that morning; now it was soaked in tears.

"Girls, look what the cat dragged in," Jasmine drawled as I walked up the driveway toward them. "Quite the look you're sporting this afternoon, Tracy. Did someone throw water on you?" The Ts' laughter was over the top. They reminded me of the flying monkeys in *The Wizard of Oz*.

Zach didn't even acknowledge me. He was lying on his back soaking up the sun. I couldn't tell what he was looking at—he was wearing mirrored sunglasses—but I assumed he was playing it cool in front of the girls.

"Zach, could you and I talk in private for a couple of minutes?" I asked. No response, but one of the Ts mimed *ooooh* with her fuchsia-pink lips.

Was he asleep? "Zach?" I said, slightly louder.

"Can't a guy rest his eyes?" he said, speaking to the sky, not to me.

I tried again. "We need to talk. Now."

"You're bothering me. Come back again when you're not—say in a decade or so."

The tittering got louder. Jasmine watched the conversation with increasing delight, her head turning from me to Zach as if she were a spectator at a tennis match. I could tell from the smirk on her face that Zach blowing me off was like Christmas Day and her birthday all rolled into one. Not only did Zach like her better, he was willing to embarrass me in front of her and her friends. I tried not to look at her face but it was nearly impossible, given how close she was sitting to Zach. She had beaten me and we both knew it.

Still, I had to get Hazel's money back, even if it meant being tortured for the next few minutes. Right now, giving back the money was the only thing I could fix, and I clung to my mission like a drowning person clinging to a floating log. I'd wanted to give Zach the opportunity to return the money in private and save him the embarrassment of being branded a thief. But if he refused to speak to me, I had no other choice.

"Zach, I mean it. We need to talk. I know you took the money."

That got everyone's attention, especially Jasmine's. The Ts looked from Zach to me and back again. Things were getting juicy.

Waiting for Zach to respond, I studied Jasmine's face. The smirk had changed into a thin line, her lips pursed so tightly they were almost white.

Zach shook his head, then propped himself up on one elbow. He kept the sunglasses on.

"I don't know what you're talking about. Stop saying stupid things."

His words were like a slap. *Stupid?* Did Zach Favola, the boy who'd hummed *Les Misérables* with me, the boy who missed his mother and who cried when his father was mean to him, the boy who wanted to work on the case with me, just call me stupid?

Zach had always sought me out, not the other way around. The Zach talking to me now was the Zach who had been so mean to Ralph. I was finally seeing the real Zach. Had every nice thing he'd ever said been a lie? My legs buckled slightly and I adjusted my footing so I wouldn't collapse. All the while, Jasmine stared at me, waiting for me to burst into tears. I didn't want to give her the satisfaction, but I could feel the cracks in my armor spreading so quickly, I was sure I'd break apart.

"She was bugging me about some money earlier, too," Jasmine said to Zach. "Tracy likes to pretend she's a detective. She's such a loser." She sang out the last word and was rewarded by her friends' laughter.

I'd known Jasmine Singh didn't like me, but I'd never known how much until that moment. I didn't think it was possible to be that mean. I could have said something equally terrible back to her, but I made a decision: I was not going to be that person. I might not have a best friend anymore and I might be grounded for the rest of my natural life, but I wasn't going to be a horrible person. I'd leave the cruelty to Jasmine and Zach and the Ts.

But she didn't know me anymore. Not really. And I didn't know her.

But I did know one thing for certain: Jasmine Singh was a bully. She didn't start out that way, but she had turned into one somewhere along the way. And I hated bullies more than anything. I might feel like an idiot for allowing Zach to fool me. I might be upset because I'd ruined my friendship with Ralph. But there was no way I was going to allow Jasmine to make me feel small ever again.

"Shut up, Jasmine. I do not still play with Barbies, but even if I did, who cares? At least I'm not mean like you. The money Ralph and I found belongs to your aunt. You might not care if she gets it back, but I do. And, Zach—you didn't seem to find me boring the last few days when we were talking about New York City and humming musicals together."

One of the Ts giggled and got a warning look from Jasmine.

Zach snorted, but he got to his feet. "I just need to talk to her, then send her on her way. Give me a second, okay Jasmine? If not, we'll be stuck listening to her yammer on all day."

"You're wasting your time, Zach," she said. "Tracy Munroe always believes she's right, no matter what."

Zach grabbed my elbow and propelled me in the direction of the garage. We stepped inside, greeted by the stale greasy smell of cars and bicycles mixed with the tang of freshly mown grass on his boots and the lawn mower.

Zach rested his arms on its handle, looking furious. "Why are you doing this to me?" he demanded.

"I'm not doing anything. Give back the money you took from the Big Rock."

"I don't know what you're talking about. I've never been to this rock. Go home and hang out with your friends and do whatever baby stuff kids like you do. But stop pretending you're a detective. You can't even solve how to dress properly."

That stung.

"I know you took the money, Zach. I won't tell Hazel. Just give it back to me."

Something shifted then. It was like I'd cornered him, and he came out swinging.

"I never liked you, Tracy. Jasmine and her Aunt Hazel had told me how silly you are. I don't know anything about any money. You're lying to try and get me in trouble. It sounds to me like *you* stole Hazel's money. I bet you spent it on ugly clothing and wooden spoons for your boyfriend, Ralph. Run along home and find that freckle you call a brother and good old Ralph. Maybe you can have a tea party in the woods."

"I want the money," I said. "I'm not leaving without it."

"Stop stalking me. Do you know how embarrassed I felt when you got my dad to bring you where I was working? And I was embarrassed for you, too. Quit acting like such a little kid."

"I wasn't stalking you! I thought you wanted me to keep you up to date on the case!" I protested.

"There is no case."

I'd been wrong to think it would be better talking to Zach in private. Waves of nausea threatened to bring me to my knees. Zach had never liked me. And it was my word against his and Jasmine's when it came to the money. I knew who Hazel was going to believe, and there was nothing I could do about it.

My eyes began to water so much that Zach looked like he was underwater. "I'm telling Hazel and your dad everything."

Zach leaned in close, so close I flinched, afraid he might hit me. When he spoke, I could barely hear him. "Listen to me, Tracy. You keep your mouth shut. I didn't take your money, and if you don't stop accusing me, I'm going to call the cops. Just because you found a candy wrapper up there doesn't mean a thing. I gave your brother one of those candy bars. Maybe you should check and see if *he* stole your money."

I couldn't breathe. Was there any chance Lester had the money? Had I messed up again? *Do* not *cry*, I told myself. I stumbled out of the garage and headed for the street. I didn't have to turn around to know that Jasmine and the Ts would have triumphant looks on their faces.

Zach followed me out. "Keep your mouth shut, Tracy, or you'll be sorry."

I gulped, only it sounded like a hiccup, which made the Plastic peanut gallery laugh even harder. I ran. I needed to get home. I needed to check with Lester. I didn't believe he'd taken the bag, but I had to be certain. Hazel was waiting for me to bring her the money and I didn't know what she would do if I didn't. But Lester would help me make a plan.

I was almost to the street when I heard Zach call my name. "Tracy, wait a minute!"

I drew in a breath. Here it was, the moment of redemption, the moment he'd prove that everything he'd said was just a show for Jasmine and her awful friends.

"Yes?" I turned around, my face full of hope.

"Don't bug me anymore."

And with those four words, Zach sliced and diced and served me up on a platter to Jasmine and her friends.

♉ ♉ ♉

I walked blindly for several blocks, wiping my eyes, trying to pull myself together. The longer I walked, the
more I knew only one person could help me: Ralph.
Sure he was mad, but he'd get over it. We'd bickered
about stuff before, hadn't we? One time, I hadn't talked
to him for a whole day when he'd teased me about
Jasmine beating me in a spelling bee when I had mis-
spelled *fashion*. It was kind of funny, since I thought
about growing up to be a fashion designer, but it didn't
seem funny at the time. Then Ralph had apologized
and we'd made up. We'd make up again.

I walked past his house several times before I got
up the nerve to knock. In the end, I pretended I was
Ingrid Bergman in the movie *Casablanca*, coming to ask
Humphrey Bogart for forgiveness. That made me feel
better, because he did forgive her in the end, just like
I was sure Ralph would forgive me. It seemed to take
forever before I heard his familiar heavy steps coming
down the hallway. When Ralph saw it was me, he turned
away. I knocked harder. Shoulders heaving, he exhaled
and turned back. The door opened, but only a crack.

"What do you want?"

Everything came out in a jumble. I was so afraid that he'd slam the door in my face before I got it all out. "I'm sorry and I feel terrible and I wanted to tell you that and I went to find Zach and it turns out he hates me and he told me that in front of Jasmine and he won't give back the money and I don't know what to do."

I waited for a flicker of sympathy, an acknowledgment of my apology and my pain. Instead, Ralph stared at me, stone-faced.

I decided to try again. "Please forgive me. I need your help." My eyes stung as I tried to blink back the tears, but there they were again. I watched Ralph's face, waiting for him to forgive me.

At least another minute passed without any response. Finally, out of desperation I blurted out, "Aren't you going to say something?"

"Good-bye." The door slammed in my face.

I stood there, stunned, and then reached for the doorknob to steady myself. I had been wrong. Ralph and I were really done. He had looked at me the same way Jasmine looked at me—with loathing.

Broken, I ran home.

CHAPTER 19

I hadn't realized I'd cried myself to sleep, but about an hour later, someone was shaking my arm.

"There you are," Mom said. "I didn't even realize you were home. Were you taking a nap?"

I nodded. The house had been empty when I'd arrived home after my run-ins with Zach and Ralph. The weight of the world on my shoulders, I'd limped up the stairs, peeled off the now completely soaked dress, and put on my pajamas. I'd crawled into bed, my whole body aching.

I was tired of thinking. All I wanted to do was get away from the wreck I'd made of my life.

Mom must have sensed something was wrong,

because she put a hand on my forehead. "You're not hot, but you look very pale. Is everything okay?"

I wanted to tell her everything, but I couldn't seem to get the words out. Nothing was okay. And it would only get worse before it got better, because I still had to face Hazel and tell my parents everything. Mom would be furious when she found out we'd found fifteen hundred dollars and hadn't turned it in. Would she feel sorry for me when I told her about Ralph hating me? Maybe. Or maybe she'd think I deserved everything I was getting.

But since I wasn't ready to talk, I put on my game face. "I just have a little headache. Maybe you could send Lester in? He's good at taking my mind off things." The funny thing was, as soon as I said it, I knew it was true.

Mom got a funny look on her face. "I thought Lester was with you and Ralph?"

This, and a flash of lightning, jolted me to sitting. Where was Lester? The lightning was followed by a crashing roll of thunder. Lester hated thunderstorms. *Think, Tracy, think.* Maybe he'd caught up with Ralph.

As soon as I thought of it, I knew it had to be true. Of course Lester was with Ralph. They were probably talking about how awful I was right now.

"Sorry. I was confused from my nap. Yes, he's with Ralph."

"Do you mind calling Ralph and telling him you won't be over until the storm lets up?"

I looked at her, blank-faced. Why would she think I was going over to Ralph's? He hated my guts. Then I remembered—she didn't know that yet.

"Tracy, you seem completely out of it," Mom said. "You do remember that Dad and I are going out to dinner with Johnny and Evelyn? I told you this morning."

I didn't remember, but nodded anyway.

"We're leaving as soon as your dad comes home and gets changed. Hazel's talk about going to the Algonquin reminded me that it's been a while since we went out for supper. It was so nice of Ralph's mother to invite you and Lester over there for the evening."

This was bad. I was going to be stuck at Ralph's for hours. It would be torture. The mention of Hazel's name only added to the speed of my already racing heart. What if she called before Mom and Dad went out, wondering why I wasn't back with the money yet?

Mom left to do her makeup and I did some quick mental calculations. Mom and Dad would be gone for at least a few hours. There was still a chance to make things right, but how?

First I had to call Ralph and make sure Lester was there. I pulled out my phone and hit the shortcut key for Ralph's number. It rang six times before the message kicked in: "Hey, this is Ralph. I'm busy saving the world right now, but if you need saving, leave me your name and number and I'll call. Yo!"

Beep. "Ralph, this is Tracy and I know you hate me now, and I wouldn't call if I didn't have to, but I don't know where Lester is. Is he over there with you?"

I waited three minutes and was just about to try his mom's number when the phone beeped.

He's not here. I haven't seen him since this morning.

I don't know where he is, I texted back. **If he shows up there, call me. Please.**

Should I go look for him?

After everything that had happened, Ralph was still willing to help. I snuffled back tears.

Not yet. I'll let you know. Thanks. And sorry. For everything. You were right about it all. I was so stupid.

I hit SEND and waited. There was no response. Ralph wasn't offering to help find Lester because of me. He was offering to help find Lester for Lester's sake. I gulped back another sob and got up, padding into Lester's bedroom, or as the sign on his door said: WELCOME TO THE MAN CAVE.

I stepped over the dirty socks and action figures and Legos that were strewn like land mines across the floor, making my way toward his desk. Nothing looked out of place.

I was hopping from empty spot to empty spot to make my way back out when something yellow sitting on Lester's bed caught my eye. I disregarded my safety precautions and was promptly rewarded by stepping on the edge of a Lego. Yelping, I hobbled to the bed and reached for the yellow object. It was the phone book, partially hidden under some dirty socks. I shoved those aside in disgust.

He had bookmarked a page with another dirty sock—yuck. The page was the Cs, and using my index finger, I went up one row of names and then down the next, hoping something would jump out at me. On the opposite-facing page I stopped: *Cogswell.* Lester had circled the name with a purple crayon. Someone had mentioned that name to me recently, but who?

I closed my eyes and tried to remember the voices of everyone I'd talked to over the last couple of days: Hazel, Mom, Lester, Zach, Ralph, Joe, Jasmine. Then it hit me. I could even remember what Mr. Favola had said: *Oh wait. He could be out on the Ledge Road, too. He's supposed to paint a shed at some place called the Cogswell Farm.* Could Lester have gone to the Cogswell Farm? And if so, why?

I couldn't quite figure it out. Now that I knew Lester hadn't been with Mom, I knew he and I must have been just missing each other all afternoon. If he wasn't home and he wasn't with Ralph, this was my only clue to his whereabouts. I was going to have to go to the Cogswell Farm.

The Ledge Road was almost a mile away. Lester wasn't allowed to bike that far. Apart from the distance, there was too much traffic and he wasn't the strongest biker yet. I pictured his little legs peddling as fast as they could along the side of the busy road. What if something had happened to him?

On his night table, beside the hockey puck he'd caught the winter before at the Boston Bruins game, was a photograph of the two of us at Old Orchard Beach, our arms around each other's shoulders, mugging for the camera and eating pink clouds of cotton candy. He looked so small. And I had been so mean to him the last time we'd spoken. If anything happened to him, I'd never forgive myself. I heard a sound at the door and looked up. Charlie was standing there staring at me. She looked annoyed, or was that just my guilty conscience? And if she was upset, who could blame her?

"Don't worry," I said, trying to sound positive. "I'll find him." She didn't appear convinced.

I took a deep breath. I'd wrecked my friendship with

Ralph, Zach had played me for a fool and blown me off in front of my archenemy, and I'd completely messed up the mystery of the paper bag in the dugout. But as bad as all those things were, they were nothing compared to the fact that my little brother's life might be in danger. I was seriously in the running for the title of worst person in the history of St. Stephen.

Maybe Jasmine was right. Maybe I did always think I was right and want things my own way. That was going to stop right now. I couldn't change the past, but I could change the future, and I could change me. And to do that, I had to put Lester first.

CHAPTER 20

As I rose to leave, I couldn't help but look up at the ceiling, which was covered in cheap plastic stars and planets. At night, the Lester Planetarium—featuring his favorite constellation, Lester Minor, a bunch of plastic stars clustered around his picture—was magical, glowing in the darkness. In the daytime, even in the gloomy light of a July thunderstorm, the constellations looked like what they were: cheap pieces of plastic stuck on the ceiling. Kind of like what Zach had turned out to be.

Zach. I was all cried out about him and now I was starting to get angry. I'd replayed the scene of him blowing me off in front of Jasmine and the Ts again and again. Each time I did, I tried to think of something—anything—else. I was sick of reliving the horrible things he and Jasmine had said to me. I wished I'd been sassier, stuck up for myself more. I thought of how Hazel must have felt when her husband left her. I'd said stupid things about that to hurt her feelings, just like Jasmine and the Ts had hurt mine. We weren't really that different were we, me and the Plastics?

Ralph has been right—I was an idiot.

My phone buzzed. *Maybe it's Lester!* I thought, though, rationally, there was no way it could be. He didn't have a phone.

Lester home yet? Ralph might hate me, but he still cared about Lester.

No, but I know where he is and I'm going to go get him.

Need help?

Every fiber in my body was shouting, *Yes, I need help!* But my fingers typed: **No, I have to do this myself.**

Okay. Let me know when he's home safe.

'K.

It was my mess and my responsibility to fix it. I

jumped over the land mines and ran to my room, where I changed out of my pajamas into jeans, a T-shirt, a pair of rubber boots, and my raincoat. The walkie-talkie Lester had given me earlier was sitting on my dresser. Lester had been so excited that morning when he'd handed it to me. Out of a sense of loyalty that I should have had over the last few days, I felt compelled to bring it along and stuck it in the pocket of my raincoat. With steely determination, I knew I was going to find my brother and bring him home.

"Did you talk to Lester?" Mom asked as I walked through the kitchen. "Dad and I are going out soon."

"Yup," I said. It seemed all I did well these days was lie. "I'm biking over there now. Have fun at dinner."

Mom looked out the window. The rain was still coming down in sheets. There was a small crash of thunder. She surveyed me and my rain gear. "Your father and I could drop you over there before we go to dinner. I'm not sure it's safe to be out biking in this weather."

"It's like, half a block, Mom. I'll be fine."

Mom continued to look doubtful, but our conversation was interrupted by the telephone ringing.

"Oh hi, Evelyn. Yes, it's terrible, isn't it? I think I'm going to wear my red dress . . ." This was my chance. I gave Mom a quick kiss on the cheek and waved as I walked out the door. She nodded absently as she continued to discuss whether Evelyn should wear her blue dress or a black suit.

The rain was almost horizontal as I biked in the direction of the Ledge Road. It was in my eyes, my nose, dripping down my face, and under my jacket soaking through my T-shirt. I felt like a character in *Moby Dick* or *The Perfect Storm*. This wasn't a rain storm; it was a typhoon. Lightning illuminated the sky in the distance. I tried counting between the flashes of lightning and the cracks of thunder like Dad had taught me—one-Mississippi, two-Mississippi—trying to determine how far away I was from the center of the storm. I couldn't remember if five or seven Mississippis equaled a mile. The storm was either two or three miles away. But, of course, Dad had failed to share a crucial piece of information—how could you tell which direction the storm was heading? Was I biking toward it, or away?

When I turned onto the Ledge Road the traffic was

noticeably lighter—just the odd set of car headlights flashing through the torrential rain like lighthouse beacons. Windshield wipers slid back and forth at their highest setting in a useless attempt to give their drivers a glimpse of the road through the wall of water. The lack of visibility and the slippery road made biking treacherous. The narrow shoulder was covered with loose gravel that gave way to a deep ravine, and as I biked on, I kept glancing down to the right, terrified that I might find Lester in a heap below.

I didn't know the Cogswell Farm. The address in the phone book said 687 Ledge Road and I counted impatiently as the house numbers slowly climbed toward 600. Finally, after fifteen minutes of terrible uphill biking and frustrating number watching, I was there. I looked up toward the house, which stood high on a hill overlooking the St. Croix River. The old white farmhouse with faded red shutters was completely dark. In fact, it looked deserted. And then I noticed the FOR SALE sign nearby.

I climbed off my bike and walked it about halfway up the driveway, where I laid it gently on the grass.

The abandoned feeling about the property was over-whelming, especially in the thunderstorm, making it seem more like a haunted house than a sweet farm. I wondered if working here had given Zach the creeps, not that I really cared anymore. Thinking of Zach reminded me of my task.

"Lester!" I hollered. As I walked up the driveway I looked all over, checking for signs of his bicycle. There were none. *Maybe he didn't come here after all,* I thought. *Maybe he thought about it and changed his mind.* But if he wasn't here, where was he?

I circled around the house, picking my way carefully through the high grass. I peeked in the windows. The house was completely empty. It looked sad and lonely.

"Lester!" I hollered again, but my voice was carried away by the howling wind and drummed out by the boom of a thunderclap.

The whole place was giving me the heebie-jeebies. I walked toward the barn, but that was too much, even for me. It was dark gray and looked like it hadn't seen a lick of paint for a hundred years. In fact, it looked like it was about to fall down at any moment. The shingles seemed like they were in a race to slide into the grass below. The more I looked at the building, the more it seemed as though the ground was in the process of swallowing the barn whole. I checked around the other side. Zach's dad said he was painting a shed. Where was it? I spun, calling Lester's name over and over.

I saw the shed down in a stand of trees. I ran toward it, somehow certain that I'd find Lester huddled beside it or inside, waiting out the storm. Unlike the barn, the shed looked sweet and well cared for, a pretty white-shingled building with the same red shutters as the house, newly painted, thanks to Zach, I guessed. The door was ajar and I flung it wide, only to find myself staring into a small and very empty room. No Lester.

My theory was a bust. Lester had probably remembered we were supposed to be at Ralph's house and was already sitting at the Huffman table, eating whatever new concoction Ralph had whipped up.

I climbed back up the hill. The storm was easing up a little. Instead of titanic waves of water, I was merely being bombarded by sailboat-sized ones. Although I couldn't tell from the overcast sky, I knew it would be twilight soon. I needed to get going. But what if Lester wasn't at Ralph's or at home? I'd have to call Mom and Dad and confess everything and they'd have to call out the National Guard. I didn't know if we even had a National Guard, but if we didn't, we should. Lester deserved nothing less.

Walking around the barn back toward the driveway, my boot caught in an abandoned piece of equipment and I fell forward. Nothing was hurt except for my dignity, and as I worked to extract my boot from an old metal loop, I thought I heard something. I held my breath, listening. Nothing. And then a deafening crash of thunder, and in the distance, a dog barking.

I scolded myself. The thunder and creepy house were making me think I was hearing things. Once my foot was free, I stood up and began to make my way more carefully around the barn. Another crash—the storm was getting closer again. Then, a crackle from my coat pocket.

I reached in and pulled out the walkie-talkie, and pressed the button. "Lester, it's me, Tracy!" A second later, the little red light came on indicating that I was getting reception, and I heard another crackle. I tried several more times, but . . . zilch. Maybe I was picking up some random cell signal. Thinking it was Lester was too good to be true.

Shoving the walkie-talkie back into my pocket, I picked up my pace and came around the front of the barn just in time to see a bolt of lightning flash from the sky and touch down near the river below. I screamed and backed up against the barn door. There was no way I was biking home now. Another flash, and I flung the door open wide and stepped into the darkness. Everything instantly became quieter.

I breathed a sigh of relief and then heard: "Have you come to let me out?"

CHAPTER 21

I jumped so high it was a miracle that I didn't bang my head on the barn roof.

"Lester?" I asked the darkness.

"Tracy?" was the confused reply, and then a frantic "Tracy! I'm trapped! Help me!"

I reached into my pocket, switched on the flashlight app on my phone, and shined it in the direction where I thought my brother's voice had come from. The light swept the room, making creepy shadows, until it caught the ghostlike face of Lester, peering down over the side of the hayloft, at least ten feet above me.

"What are you doing up there?"

Lester began to cry, huge racking sobs of fear and maybe relief that I was there. Every time he tried to stop and speak they would start up again.

"It was Zach," he said when he finally caught his breath.

"What do you mean *It was Zach?* Tell me everything while I try to figure out a way to get you down." I scanned the room looking for a ladder.

"After you left, I saw Zach going down the tracks toward the Junkyard, and it made me suspicious, so I followed him. He took the money!"

A wave of relief passed over me. I had a witness! It wasn't my word against Zach's anymore!

"Then I followed him to the Garcelons', but people kept coming, first Jasmine and her friends, and then—"

"Me," I finished. I was circling below, trying to figure out how he'd gotten up into the hayloft. "I'm so sorry I was mean to you earlier. You were right. I was scared to go see Hazel. And you were right about me wanting to drive around in Mr. Favola's car, and you were right about me being an idiot for working with Zach. I hope you can forgive me."

"Sure I can. Where's Ralph anyway?"

"He found out about Zach."

My brother gave a little squeak, but had the good sense not to say anything. "Listen to me, Lester. Stay back from the edge, okay? It's dark and you're up really high. I don't want you to fall and break your neck. I'm trying to find the ladder."

I could hear the rustle of straw as Lester moved back from the edge. "There is no ladder," he called from the blackness above.

"What do you mean, there's no ladder? How'd you get up there?"

"Zach used a ladder, but it's gone."

"He took it away?" I was getting sicker by the minute. What kind of person was Zach anyway? It was one thing to be mean to me, but to hurt Lester? That was unforgivable.

"Yeah, I overheard him tell those stupid girls that he had to go to the Cogswell Farm on the Ledge Road, so I ran home, looked up the address, and biked here. I wanted to confront him after how mean he was to you—someone has to defend your honor—and when

I did he got real mad and hauled me in here. Then he shoved me over to the ladder and said he would beat me up if I didn't go up into the hayloft."

"He said he would beat you up?" I felt like a parrot, but it was so horrible I couldn't help but repeat what Lester was saying.

"Uh-huh. I tried to use the Silly String on him, but I missed. When I got to the top, Zach took the ladder and moved it over to the opposite wall so I couldn't reach it. Then he said, 'Let's see how you like being up there.'"

My hands clenched into fists at my side. I had never hit anybody in my life, but I wanted to hurt Zach Favola. I couldn't wait to tell my parents and Hazel what he had done to Lester. I was sure that Zach was about to experience the same kind of misery he'd put Lester through.

"Then he left and it began to thunder and lightning and things were moving around in the hayloft and it got dark and I started to scream for help. I'd scream for a while and then take a break. I kept using my inhaler to keep calm until Zach came back. But he didn't come back. No one did until you came to save me." Lester took a deep shaky breath.

"How long have you been up there?"

"A couple of hours, I think. I really have to go to the bathroom. I couldn't pee over the side. It was too dark and I thought I might fall."

I whirled around behind me and shined the light on the opposite wall. I couldn't see a ladder there.

"Lester, I don't see anything on the other side of the barn. Are you sure that's where he put it?"

"Yeah, but when Zach left he slammed the barn door and I heard the ladder fall over. I heard it smash on the floor."

I swung my phone toward the ground. The ladder lay broken into dozens of pieces. Looking at the debris, it was a miracle it hadn't broken when Lester had climbed up into the loft. The wood was so brittle it looked like even I could have snapped it in half. I walked over and picked up a piece of the wood. It fell apart in my hand. An image of Lester falling in the darkness planted itself in my mind. I had to take a few deep breaths to calm myself. I flashed the light around the room again, checking every corner and shadow for another ladder. There wasn't one.

"It's too dark when you take the flashlight off me!" Lester cried. "I can't see you!"

I shined the light back up toward him. "Lester, breathe. I'm checking for a light switch, okay? I won't leave you. But you can't move. You might fall."

He made a kind of gulpy sound, which I took as an okay, and I turned my phone back toward the barn door. There, to the right, was a tarnished switch plate. I stepped across and flipped the switch. Nothing.

"The power must be out because of the storm."

"What will you do?" Lester's voice sounded far away.

"I'm going to call for help." I pushed a button to exit the flashlight app, and then punched the button for Mom's cell phone. Nothing happened. I had no bars.

"There's no coverage in here. I'm going to step outside and try in the yard, okay?"

"You can't go!"

I turned the flashlight on again and shined it up at him. "Listen to me, Lester: We're going to get through this, okay? Remember how nervous you were when we went to Old Orchard Beach? You survived that, didn't you? After you got used to it, you had a good time, even if you were allergic to most of it."

Lester said nothing.

"And you were brave enough to become part of our detective team, weren't you? You helped us talk to people and you learned to climb up the Big Rock, and you had a lot of good ideas, didn't you?"

"Yes . . ."

"So you got this, okay? Everything will be fine! I promise. I just need to step outside and see if my phone works out there."

"You're going to come right back?"

"Of course I'm coming back!"

"Could you leave the door open?"

That was a good idea. I opened the barn door, but it kept swinging closed from the combination of its weight and the high winds. I looked around for something to prop it open with and finally found a crate. It took me a few minutes to drag it over and shove it against the open door, but immediately, the inkiness of the barn was replaced by a wash of pale light. Though it was still pretty dim inside, I could see Lester clearly now, as well as all of the old equipment. It looked like the barn hadn't been used in a long time.

"I'm going to step out into the driveway, Lester. Don't move. That hayloft doesn't look safe."

He nodded and watched as I went outside and began punching numbers into my phone again. Still no bars.

"The storm must have done something to the cell coverage," I said, coming back inside. "I can't call anyone or send a text. Ralph's mom must be wondering where we are. We were supposed to be there an hour ago. I'm going to have to bike down the road to the next house and see if they can call the police or take me to Ralph's. Mom and Dad are in St. Andrews having dinner."

"No! You can't leave me! You need to get me down. There are creepy-crawlies up here. I felt something move a few minutes ago. I want to go home, *now!*" Lester's voice was no longer bordering on hysterical. He was in full-on-panic mode.

I looked around but still couldn't see any way to get him down. Then I noticed the block and tackle hanging on a long rod that ran perpendicular to the hayloft on the wall. It was meant to move bales of hay between the hayloft and the ground. Could I somehow use that to get my brother down? I stared at the mechanism for several minutes and then the solution came to me.

"I'm coming up to get you," I said, crossing the floor.

"How?"

By now I was at the wall, looking up. The hayloft was only ten feet off the ground, but it might as well have been a hundred. I felt faint seeing how high I was going to have to climb.

"Physics."

CHAPTER 22

I could thank my fourth-grade science teacher, Mr. Johnson, and Ralph for what little I understood about blocks and tackles. Our class had been divided into teams of two and assigned a project about how the laws of physics were used to help people in everyday life when they didn't have access to fancy machinery or equipment. Ralph's uncle worked for a moving company in Chicago, where they often had to move big pieces of furniture like pianos or king-sized beds into apartments by hoisting them up and through big windows using pulleys and ropes. My team had built a miniature block and tackle and moved heavy blocks into a large Lego building using our pinky fingers. We'd gotten an A on our project.

The barn's block and tackle was as simple as the one we'd made, just bigger. The large metal hook from which the pulley hung was attached so it could move back and forth along a fifteen-foot-long rod; only right now it was pulled as far away from the hayloft as it could be. The rope on the right of the pulley hung all the way to the ground, with a large knot tied at the bottom so that it could never be pulled all the way through. The hook was on the other, shorter, end of the rope. If I could figure out some way to attach myself to the rope on the right, I could pull the rope on the left and easily haul myself to the top. Lester could climb onto me and we could lower ourselves back to the ground. Easy-peasy.

Pulling on the rope, I moved the block and tackle along until it was as close to the hayloft as it would go. But I couldn't figure out how to attach myself to the rope. When I tried to stand on the knot my feet kept slipping off. I tried to climb it instead and got exactly nowhere. For some reason I had forgotten that, like Lester, I didn't have an athletic bone in my body. What

I really needed was some kind of seat to sit in like I saw the Coast Guard use on TV when they rescued people who fell off their boats. I had no idea how to make one, but I knew someone who did.

"Lester, when your summer camp went to Cape Enrage last summer, didn't you rappel down a cliff?"

Lester looked at me as if he thought this was a very strange time to be discussing his field trip. "Yes . . ."

"Did they show you how they made seats out of rope when they need to save someone?"

"Yeah, but I'm not sure I can remember what they said. Why don't you Google it?"

"No bars, remember? If we're going to get you down, we're going to have to do it without the help of all of the brains in the universe. We're going to have to rely on our *own* brains."

Lester sat back on his heels. "I don't know, Tracy. I don't remember."

"Think! You're so good with mechanical things. Tell me what to do, and I'll do it. Do you want to get down from there and go home or not? You either have to remember, or I have to go out in the storm and get help." I glanced outside over my shoulder. It was still raining hard, though there hadn't been a flash of lightning for about ten minutes.

"Okay, okay, let me think."

Rather than standing there making him nervous, I wandered around the barn giving him some room. It smelled like hay and damp fur and old wood, but I kind of liked it. On the wall near the door was an old calendar: Dewolfe Hardware, 1975. I wondered why someone would keep such an old calendar. The picture was faded and looked almost like an old painting—the colors were all washed out—but it was fun to see the old cars parked in front of the store. Dewolfe Hardware had closed long before I was born, but it looked like the kind of place I would have loved to shop.

"I remember!" Lester called down. "It's called a Swiss seat!"

"Great. How do I make it?" I looked up, waiting for instructions.

"You take the rope," he began and then stopped. "Argh! You need to be able to use both ends of the rope. If you pull more rope down, you won't be able to haul yourself back up. The seat takes a lot of rope. It's got to go around your waist and legs a couple of times and then be knotted real tight."

I grabbed the rope and tried to do what Lester suggested but he was right—by the time I followed the instructions and had myself encased in rope, it was completely impossible to reach the hook on the other side. I untied myself and plopped back on the floor, defeated.

"It was a good idea," Lester offered, his voice quavering. "Do you want a piece of licorice? I was rationing it in case I was stuck in here for weeks."

As soon as he said licorice, I remembered Lester riffling through his knapsack that morning, as clearly as if it were a movie being projected on the wall. I saw Silly String, walkie-talkies, a notebook, licorice, and a rope.

"The rope!" I cried. "Lester, do you still have that long yellow rope in your knapsack?"

"I forgot about the rope!" he shouted. "After Zach left I thought about tying the rope to something up here and trying to climb down, but I couldn't find anything to tie it to and I was too scared I might fall. I'm not very strong you know. . . ."

"Well I can use it. Throw it to me!" A second later a long yellow coil landed with a thump on the floor beside me. Lester talked me through the complicated knots to create the Swiss seat and how to firmly attach our family's new clothesline to the old rope. When I was done, I pulled with all my might. Everything held. Time to go get Lester!

I was okay at first, but about five feet off the ground, I began to feel woozy. Despite my gentle hand-over-hand technique, my seat was swinging from side to side. And when I looked down? That was the worst. I pictured all kinds of scenarios, and they all ended the same way: me crashing to the barn floor and breaking my neck.

I stopped hauling and hung there, taking deep breaths and trying to think of anything other than the fact that I was hanging on very dubiously tied ropes without a net to catch me. I started back down.

"What's wrong?" Lester called out.

I looked up at his anxious face and shook my head. "I'm sorry. I don't think I can do this. It's so high. What if I fall? What if we fall? I feel just like I did on the Ferris wheel at Old Orchard Beach. I think I might faint."

"Tracy, you're safe. You've tied these as well as any ropes I saw the guides tie at Cape Enrage. I know you're scared of heights, but I'm scared of dark places and creepy-crawly things and I want to go home." *Home* came out as a wail.

I took another breath and closed my eyes. This time, instead of imagining us crashing to our untimely deaths, I pictured us on the ground, high-fiving, fist pumping, hugging. I imagined telling Ralph all about my daring rescue and how impressed he'd be and how he'd forgive me on the spot because I'd been so brave. I opened my eyes and began climbing again.

In no time at all, I was eye-level with Lester. The air was mustier the higher I went—and hotter. Lester was lucky it hadn't been a sweltering day. The hayloft would have been broiling in that kind of weather and the heat would have triggered his asthma.

At the very top, I reached for a wooden beam and was able to pull myself over so that I was actually sitting on the edge of the loft. "Okay, climb on and hold tight."

Just as Lester began to edge himself in my direction,

something darted from the pile of hay behind him. We both screamed and the thing yowled and hurled itself in my direction. I imagined a rat or a raccoon or a hibernating bear and clung to the wooden beam for dear life. The thing kept coming, hidden by piles of hay and screeching like a banshee, although, to be honest, it was impossible to tell where its screams started and ours ended.

"It's a monster!" Lester shouted, scooting as fast as he could in my direction. I held out my arms toward him, but just as I was about to grab him, something black and furry jumped into my arms instead. I screamed. The thing did, too. I was about to drop it when I realized it was a black-and-white cat.

"It's a kitten!" I shouted.

"Mrow," the kitten murmured, as if this was just a normal day in the barn. And then Lester and I both began to laugh hysterically, all the way through him climbing into my lap and wrapping his arms around my neck, all the way back down to the ground, and all the way through untying the elaborate knots. We were still laughing as we walked out of the barn, the kitten following happily behind us, until a steamroller of a thunderclap passed over us and Lester began to sob uncontrollably.

"C'mon," I said, putting an arm around his shoulder. "I'll double you on my bike. Where's your bike anyway? I didn't see it when I got here."

"That's because it's down in the ditch."

"How did it get in the ditch?" I pictured the cars I'd passed on the way to the farm and how I knew they couldn't see me well because of the storm. Thinking of Lester's bike in the ditch made me feel sick again.

He sounded much calmer than me. "Oh, I fell off it going around a turn and the bike tumbled in. I couldn't get it out by myself. Dad's going to have to come back with me."

Mom and Dad. How was I going to explain all of this to them?

"Okay, hop on. Oh wait, you should probably go pee out behind the barn first."

"I don't need to now," he said, proudly.

"How come? Did you go up in the hayloft?" I was pretty sure I hadn't felt anything wet when I'd brought him down.

"No. I just decided maybe I didn't need to go to the bathroom after all, that I need to learn to hold it in, even when I'm nervous."

I climbed onto my bike and Lester arranged himself awkwardly on the carrier that was attached to the back of the seat. As we rolled down the long driveway I could feel his whole body shudder.

"You saved my life."

"You tried to defend my honor."

"I can't believe you climbed up to get me. It was amazing."

"I'm kind of amazed myself."

"Do you think your fear of heights is gone now? Ralph told me they have a Ferris wheel at the Exhibition in Fredericton."

I shrugged. "Maybe." And then the sensation of the chair rounding the top of the Ferris wheel returned. I shook my head. "Nope. I think I'll stay on the ground. Unless you need saving."

"I won't."

I smiled. The two of us were quiet the rest of the way home.

CHAPTER 23

After I deposited a still nose- and eye-dripping Lester
in his room, I began to pace my bedroom. What Zach
had done to Lester was unforgivable. It was one thing
to be a thief, or to make fun of me in front of Jasmine
and her friends. But scaring the snot (literally) out of a
little kid like Lester put Zach in the supervillain cate-
gory in my books.

I marched into the bathroom and began to fill the
tub with water. Mom's lavender bath salts sat on the
shelf over the toilet. *Relieves Stress*, the box said. I
wasn't sure how much to add so I tossed in half the
container. If anyone needed stress relieved, it was
Lester. As the tub filled, the air became perfumed with

what was supposed to—according to the package—be the scent of a thousand lavender plants in the south of France, but which seemed more like the sickly smell of a thousand air fresheners. When the water reached the line of dirt from my bath of the night before, I turned the faucet off and knocked on Lester's door.

He stuck his head out. In the dim hallway light his face reminded me of the-man-in-the-moon night-light that was plugged into the socket outside his door.

"I think I'm going to go to bed," he said, pointing down at his pajamas and bathrobe and then toward the bed behind him.

"You should take a bath," I said. "It'll calm you down and help you sleep. I even added some of Mom's lavender salts. They'll help you feel better."

For a second, it seemed that he was going to protest, but then he nodded and shuffled off toward the bathroom, the striped belt of his bathrobe trailing behind him like a long tail. I heard a quiet slap of water as he climbed in, and then all was quiet again. I went back to my pacing.

I remembered that I hadn't texted Ralph to let him know Lester was safe.

Lester and I are home. He's okay. When Mom and Dad get home, I'm telling them everything, and then going to see Hazel.

Ralph must have been watching his phone. **Thanks. Mom and I have been driving all over town looking for you. Mom was about to call your parents. We're on our way.**

I thought for a second and then sent Ralph one more message: **No matter what, you are always my best friend. I don't know why I was so stupid. If you can't forgive me, I understand. I don't forgive myself. But if you can, I would be really happy. See you in a couple of minutes.**

"I can't let Zach get away with this," I muttered. "I need to find that money and give it back to Hazel before Mom and Dad get home. I need to avenge Lester's honor. I'm not some stupid kid from the middle of nowhere. And if Zach thinks he's beaten me, he's in for a big surprise."

I paused for a moment and glanced out the window. The rain clouds had passed, and the sky looked like it had been scrubbed clean. There was a pinkish hue where the sun had just set.

"Red sky at night, sailor's delight," I whispered. Tomorrow would be a beautiful day.

I stared across the shrubs toward the ball field, where I could just make out the black roof of the dugout. The low lazy whistle of the evening train blew in the distance. It sounded as mournful as I felt.

Out of the corner of my eye I caught a glimpse of something moving off to my left. I turned in time to see Zach bending over to crawl under Hazel's back deck. He held something white in his hands. What was he up to? My curiosity was replaced by a stronger emotion: rage.

I stopped briefly at the bathroom door. "I have to go out for a minute!" I called.

"You're leaving me alone?" Lester sounded shocked, scared.

"I'm just going into the backyard for a second," I lied. "I saw something I need to fix. I'll be right back.

Ralph and his mom are on their way to stay with us until Mom and Dad get home."

"Come right back," Lester said. It was a demand, not a request.

"Of course I will," I called over my shoulder and took the stairs two at a time.

I slid through the small opening in the low hedge that separated our property from Hazel's, careful not to make a sound. As I emerged on the other side, I caught sight of the back of Zack's dirty T-shirt rounding the corner toward the front of Hazel's house. I thought of chasing him, then stopped myself. What if the thing he'd had in his hands was the money? I had to be sure before I confronted him.

The opening under the steps was narrow and I shuddered looking into the dark underbelly of the deck. I flipped on my flashlight app and crouched down, easing myself in as gently as I could, anxious to avoid the cobwebs and nail ends that stuck out of the underside of the steps. The air was warmer here and smelled of old wood and mud. There was a steady drip as the deck worked to dry itself. I swept the light around the crawl space, hoping to glimpse the white thing, but I couldn't see anything except for a few old boards and an empty pop can. Whatever Zach had been holding, he hadn't left it under the deck.

I began to inch my way back out when I caught sight of a bit of white plastic lodged under the steps at an angle that was impossible to see when you crawled in. I reached over and pulled it toward me. It was a plastic grocery bag wrapped around something else and taped shut. I ripped open the plastic and there it was: the infamous paper bag of money. Equal parts relief and joy washed over me. Now I could fix everything. I tucked the bag into my pocket, began to crawl back out from beneath the deck, and stood up, trying to brush the muck off my jeans.

Then I turned and bumped straight into Zach.

CHAPTER 24

"I'll take that," he demanded, holding out his hand. He was impatiently opening and closing it as if he were some kind of villain, which I guess he kind of was.

I looked from his hand up to his face, and into the green eyes that I'd once thought were so wonderful, but which now reminded me of the green sludge that collects at the bottom of the town pool when they don't use enough chlorine. Zach was no teen idol. But he wasn't a scary villain, either. He was just a dumb kid. In fact, he was so ordinary to me now that I couldn't help but laugh.

"Get over yourself, Zach." I shoved past him,

heading toward Hazel's front door. I'd caught him off guard, but only for a moment. He grabbed my arm and twisted me around to face him.

And that was his fatal error.

"Do *not* touch me!" I spat. "I'm not some little kid you can lock away in an old barn and terrify just so I won't tell on you."

Zach looked surprised for a moment, and then regained his composure. "You found him," was the simple, unapologetic response.

His sheer meanness was like a red flag to the big sister bull I'd become. I stepped forward so fast that Zach stumbled back.

"How long were you going to leave him there, huh?" I said, stabbing at Zach's chest with my finger so hard it felt like it was made of steel. "Lester's a kid. He's nine years old. What kind of monster traps a kid in an old barn during a thunderstorm? He was scared to death. I was scared to death wondering where he was. What kind of a creep are you, anyway?"

Zach's cheek twitched. "It's no big deal. I was on my way to go get him right now, honest. I only wanted to scare the kid a little so he wouldn't tell anyone that I had the money."

I shoved Zach again with my newfound superhero sister strength. "No big deal! You almost killed him! And in case you haven't noticed, it's almost dark. Can you imagine how dark it must be inside that barn right now? How scared a little kid would be, trapped in a hayloft in an old barn? Did you know the ladder broke when you slammed the door shut? Do you even care?"

Zach's eyes widened. He licked his lips and swallowed hard. "How did you get him down? Did you have to call the fire department or the police?"

"It's none of your business how I got him down, and don't worry, I'm sure the police will want to talk to you soon enough. What you did was mean and reckless; what if Lester had fallen out of the hayloft and broken his neck?"

Zach went pale. It was clear he hadn't thought his plan through. "But the kid's okay, right?"

"No thanks to you." I stepped back and surveyed him. What had I ever seen in Zach? He and Jasmine deserved each other.

"Wait till I tell Hazel and your dad and my parents what you did to my brother. It was bad enough that you stole money you knew we were trying to return to Hazel. And it was awful how cruel you and Jasmine were to me. But what you did to Lester is criminal."

Like a marionette whose strings had been snipped, Zach dropped to the ground and put his head between his knees.

"I didn't mean for any of this stuff to happen," he whispered. I couldn't tell if he was being truthful or not and frankly I didn't care. He was probably just upset because he'd gotten caught. The bad guys in old movies always felt bad when they got caught.

"If you didn't want any of this to happen, you shouldn't have stolen the money in the first place," I said. "I trusted you."

He looked up, his face defiant. "Well, you guys stole the money, too."

I shook my head in disgust. While I wasn't proud of my behavior over the last few days, I wasn't going to let him lump us in with him. "We didn't steal the money, and you know it, Zach. The only thing we're guilty of is getting too excited. You're guilty of lying and kidnapping my little brother."

"You could have turned the money in right away, Tracy. And you lied to your brother and Ralph when you didn't tell them that you agreed to let me help with the case. You're not so different from me."

He couldn't tell in the dusky light, but I had turned bright pink. The words I couldn't find earlier when he was being cruel to me were now coming freely. "I did some stupid things, but don't you dare try to bring me down to your level. And I've already paid for those mistakes; I've lost my best friend. We were excited to have a mystery to solve. We thought it would be fun. As soon as we were sure the money belonged to Hazel, we went right out to the Big Rock to get it. You, on the other hand, are a scummy thief. What did you steal the money for anyway?"

Zach leaned his head against his knees. He seemed to shrink before my eyes. "You wouldn't understand."

"Try me."

He looked up at me and took a deep breath. "Look—I feel terrible about the thing with Lester. I panicked.

He said he was going to turn me in and nothing I said seemed to make any difference to him. He kept talking about defending your honor, Ralph's honor, Hazel's honor, even the honor of St. Stephen."

I smiled. Lester was the best of us all, even in his annoying, know-it-all way. It made me feel proud to have him for a younger brother, like I suddenly understood that I was the sister of someone special, someone who was going to grow up and do amazing things. My job would be to protect him, and help him if I could.

When I didn't reply, Zach kept going. "But I had a good reason for stealing the money."

This I had to hear. "And that would be . . ."

"I want to go home to New York. I'm going to run away tonight."

"What do you mean?" I'd never known anyone who'd run away before. Except in books. In books people ran away all the time.

"I hate it here and I hate my dad," he whispered. Zach's head fell forward onto his knees again and he began to wail. "You saw what he was like today, Tracy. He's *so* mean. That's what he's always like with me.

Nothing I do is ever good enough for him. It's like I'm the worst kid in the world. He doesn't love me at all."

"Parents always love their kids," I said. I sure hoped so anyway, considering how much trouble I was about to get in.

Zach shook his head. "You think that because you have nice parents." He sounded bitter. "It's not like that in my family. My mom loves me. But my dad? My dad loves himself, his work, his girlfriends, and his fancy cars. He loves things, not people. After today, I knew I couldn't stay. It would take me too long to earn the money to leave, but Hazel's money is more than enough for a bus ticket and a couple meals along the way."

"But how did you figure out where we hid the money?"

"I followed you guys out to that rock a few days ago. I thought it would be fun to spy on you. I told you I was bored. Ralph wouldn't let me hang out with you guys—"

"Because you were mean to him," I snarled. "Maybe if you'd been nicer he'd want to be your friend."

Zach shrugged. I noticed he didn't apologize and I added that to the list of things I really disliked about him. "Anyway, all of a sudden, today it hit me. That's probably where you guys had hidden the money, so I went out and looked around. It took a while, but I found it. There's a bus leaving for New York City in about two hours. I'm going to be on it. Just give me back the money. I want to go home, Tracy. Please. Let me just go home to my mom."

"Zach, I can't do that." My voice was firm. "Right now, you're just a kid who found some money that Ralph, Lester, and I were dumb enough to hide, thinking we were protecting it. But if you buy a ticket and get on that bus, you're a thief."

Zach took his eyes off me for a moment and stared up at the sky, which was now a deep blue and had begun to sprout random stars here and there. His face was a shadow in the dim glow of the distant streetlight.

"Please, Tracy. I hate it here," was his quiet response.

"I bet you do, considering all the trouble you've caused. The answer is no. As soon as Hazel and your dad get back from their date, we're going to tell her everything."

Zach gave a nasty laugh. "There's no date. Dad blew her off. He always has a couple of girls he's seeing, and I guess one of the younger or prettier ones was suddenly available tonight. That's why I stuck the money under the deck. I was going back inside to pack a few things, and I didn't want it on me in case Hazel asked about it. I was going to slip out the window, grab the money, and go." I noted that he didn't mention saving Lester. He had never planned to rescue Lester. I added that to my list and I would definitely be sharing that with Hazel and my parents.

I pictured Hazel, all dolled up, waiting for Mr. Favola. My heart sank. She and I had both been played by the Favolas.

"Does Hazel know he's out with someone else?"

"Nah," Zach said, shaking his head. "Dad's too smooth to get caught. And I don't care anyway. Hazel's an idiot if she likes my dad."

"Just like I was an idiot for trusting you," I said. "You

were cruel today. Just like your father is cruel to you and like he's being cruel to Hazel tonight. I wonder what Jasmine would think if she knew you begged me to let you help us solve the case or that you became friends with me to make her jealous? I bet she wouldn't be very impressed. Only a sneak does those kinds of things. You and your dad use people. I don't care how much trouble you get in. You deserve it after what you've done."

Zach's eyes flashed. For a second, I thought he might lash out at me, but instead he started crying. "I'm nothing like my dad," he whispered.

"Zach, you're exactly like your dad." He cowered like the coward he was. "And you can't go back to New York until you talk to your mom and dad and make things right with Hazel, Lester, and Ralph. You need to face up to your mistakes. So do I. And, for the record, I think you need to tell your dad how unhappy you are."

I turned toward the door, but Zach reached out and grabbed my arm again. I spun around, ready to wrestle him for the plastic bag. Instead, I saw his anguished face. He was crying for real now and his nose had turned pink. He looked remarkably like the Lester I'd just left at home. *Lester!*

"Wait here for two minutes. I have to go check on my brother. He's home alone and he's really scared after what you did to him."

"It's okay, I'm here," Lester said, stepping out from the shadows, holding Charlie by her leash. She looked at Zach and gave a long, low growl. Lester must have told her everything. If it wasn't such a charged moment I might have laughed: Lester was wearing his Star Wars pajamas and slippers. "I could hear you and Zach arguing through the bathroom window, so I dried off and came right over in case you needed help."

"Lester, you're my hero," I said and gave him the biggest hug ever. He was turning into my knight in flannel armor. United, we turned and faced Zach. He couldn't even look at Lester, which made me think that maybe he wasn't as much of a monster as I'd thought he was. Even boy-band clones can be pathetic, I guess.

Before we went inside, there was one nagging question that I needed Zach to answer, even though I was kind of afraid to hear the response. "Did you always think I was that silly? I only wanted to be your friend. I didn't deserve to be treated like that in front of Jasmine and her crew."

Zach looked uncomfortable. "I'm sorry, Tracy," he said. "In the beginning, I wanted to be your friend because I knew it would bother Ralph and Hazel. For different reasons, obviously. And I thought it would make Jasmine jealous, which it did." He glanced over at the empty bench under the apple tree, as if he could see the two of us sitting there. "But then I got to know you, and I did like you. You're kind of a goofy kid, but in a smart, interesting way. It was fun to talk to you. You weren't trying to impress me all the time like Jasmine was. I could just be me. I know I was a real jerk to blow you off in front of those girls today, especially when I knew they didn't like you. I just wanted you to stop talking about the money in front of them, that's all." He continued to stare at the bench, unable to meet my eye.

I didn't know whether I believed Zach or not, but it sort of sounded true. I wanted it to be true, anyway. At least, the part where he'd called me smart and interesting. The goofy kid part made me feel embarrassed. All I could think about was how my friendship with Zach was based on nothing more than us both trying to make Jasmine jealous. She'd won. Just like she always did. Would I never learn?

I inched my way forward, keeping Lester close. We were only a few feet from Hazel's front door now. Her entryway was dark, but the glow from her kitchen spilled out onto the nearby grass.

"Wait!" Zach called. He sounded desperate.

I turned back to him one last time. "Zach, it's over, okay?" If he was frantic now, I was just plain tired after the evening's events. I wanted to get the whole thing over with and go home and sleep for a week.

"My dad is going to kill me!" he said. I nodded. I suspected that Mr. Favola would be furious.

"My parents aren't going to be too thrilled with me, either," I said.

Zach turned to Lester. "I can't believe I was so terrible to you," he whispered. "I'm sorry."

Lester stared at Zach, and a big tear slid down his cheek. "I was so scared," he said, and then he buried his face in my shoulder, his sobs making us both jiggle. I started to cry, too, remembering all the ways Lester's time in the hayloft could have ended in disaster.

"I know," Zach said. I could tell from the look on his face that he now genuinely felt bad. "Please tell Ralph I'm sorry, too."

"You can tell me yourself," Ralph said, coming up the driveway, his mother beside him, looking frantic that the kids she was supposed to be taking care of hadn't shown up.

"Thank goodness you're all right," she cried, pulling Lester and me in for a tight hug. "I've called your parents, and they're on their way."

I peeked at Ralph from underneath his mom's armpit. He smiled, but looked serious. "I told Mom everything. We're going in with you and Zach to talk to Hazel. I'm as responsible for everything that's happened as you." For the first time in a week, I saw the face of my best friend looking back at me. I wanted to give him a hug, but I thought it would embarrass him, so I just gave him a small smile.

But Ralph was full of surprises. "And one more

thing," he said, coming to join Lester, his mom, and me in a big group hug, "There's no reason to forgive you. I could never stay mad at you, Tracy. I should have told you about Hazel's cooking lessons right away. I know you wouldn't have said anything. I guess I just wanted to seem cool, and I thought you wouldn't think I was if you knew I was helping Hazel."

"Teaching someone to cook is cool," I said.

"I knew Ralph wouldn't stay mad!" Lester crowed. I nodded, too happy to speak. At that moment it was like the sun had come out, even though it was so dark I could barely see everyone's faces clearly. Zach stood apart from us, his head hanging low.

I untangled myself from the hug and turned back toward Zach. "We should go in now. We have a lot to talk to Hazel about. She's not going to believe all of this."

"Try me," a voice said, and suddenly the porch light flipped on, illuminating everything. I squinted as my eyes adjusted to the light, and saw Hazel and Jasmine standing in the doorway. I glanced over at Zach. He looked even more humiliated.

I couldn't read Hazel's face. "Jasmine came over a little while ago and has been filling me in on a lot of interesting things. I'm sorry to say we've been eavesdropping. Your conversation with Zach answered most of my questions, Tracy, although I do have a few more." She opened the door wide. "Come on in. We have a lot to talk about."

Together, we walked into Hazel's house to make things right.

Chapter 25

A week later I was given a slight reprieve by Mom, who agreed to let me out of the house for an hour as long as I stayed in the neighborhood.

She'd followed me to the kitchen door to give me one last set of instructions. "And I don't care if you see the most interesting or suspicious thing ever, you keep going, okay? *No more snooping!*"

It had been a long week. I was sure my parents were going to blow a gasket when they heard about the money. But that was nothing compared to the fit they had when they heard the whole story about Lester in the barn and me saving him. I might have been a hero to my brother but, to quote my dad, me using the block and tackle to rescue Lester was "reckless, irresponsible, and potentially life threatening." I'd lost count of the number of lectures we'd received and the number of chores that had been added to my list. It was bad, but it didn't seem as horrible, because at least my parents hadn't banned me from texting or calling Ralph.

Now I was on my way to meet Ralph and Lester at Brown's Store. Lester's grounding had only been for a couple of days, and Ralph was trying to keep him busy and out of my hair, which I appreciated. From our front walk, I could see Mr. Favola's fancy convertible pulling out of Hazel's driveway. I stopped and waited for it to leave, a sense of relief washing over me that Zach was finally gone. He had been right, though; his dad could be a real jerk. But I could also tell that he loved Zach, and he wanted to make things better between the two of them. The night that we'd confessed everything, Zach and his dad had stayed in Hazel's TV room for a long time talking, and when they came out, I could tell they'd both been crying. That gave me a little hope.

Now they were on their way home to New York

City. Zach was going to spend the rest of the summer with his mom, and it turned out she was really happy he'd be home again. Mr. Favola planned to stay in New York City for a while, too, so he could spend more time with Zach. Hazel told me that the Favolas were going to get family counseling to help Zach cope with the divorce and his anger; I hoped it would give him some peace and keep him out of trouble.

Of course I didn't hear any of this from Zach. He'd called a couple of times to try and apologize again but the Munroe family had made it very clear to him and his dad that we wanted nothing to do with them.

No surprise, his relationship with Jasmine had completely fizzled. Jasmine's never liked backing a loser. To be fair—and I hated to be when it came to Jasmine—I knew that she was loyal to Hazel. And I was impressed that she had done the right thing, coming to see her aunt as soon as she realized Zach had the money.

♀ ♀ ♀

The morning after that awful night, Jasmine came to

see me. I was shocked when I opened the door. She looked equally shocked to be standing there.

"Um, do you want to come in?" I asked.

She gave me a stiff nod and followed me into the house. Lester and Mom were in the kitchen trying a new recipe of Ralph's. They both raised their eyebrows when they saw who was with me. I'm sure Jasmine noticed their reaction, since she asked if there was somewhere private we could speak. I ushered her up to my room. Normally, I wouldn't share my personal space with her, afraid of the wisecracks she'd make at my expense, but nothing Jasmine could say or do could hurt me now. Maybe when someone hurts you enough, you find a way to grow a second skin so they can never get to you again.

Jasmine's eyes scanned my room, taking it all in. She reached out and lightly touched my hat rack. "You have a lot of cool hats," she said.

I nodded.

"Your room looks like you," she continued, her arm sweeping the air. "It's nice. It has a lot of personality."

I looked around for a hidden camera, expecting

someone to jump out and shout "Gotcha!" No way was Jasmine Singh paying me a compliment. I continued to sit silently, waiting to find out why she was visiting.

As if she were reading my thoughts, she nodded. "So . . . I'm here to apologize."

I waited.

"I was really mean to you yesterday. My friends were pretty terrible, too."

"Uh-huh." I wasn't going to make this easy for her.

"And I know that was wrong. You were only trying to get my Aunt Hazel's money back from Zach. I didn't know he was a thief or that he would hurt a little kid," she added, looking me directly in the eye. "I liked him. He was always nice to me. But I was mean to you because I was jealous."

"You were jealous?" I couldn't keep the surprise out of my voice. "Why would you be jealous of *me?*"

Jasmine's mouth twisted a little as she looked around my room again. "Why wouldn't I be jealous of you? Look at this room. It's so cool and interesting. *You're* so cool and interesting. Everyone thinks you're funny and smart and they like that you do your own thing and don't worry about other people's opinions."

"Not everyone."

Jasmine laughed. "No, not everyone. But most people. It's hard for me, because all of the teachers are always comparing us, and I can tell they think you're special."

"All the teachers like you, too," I countered.

"I know they like me. They think I'm smart. But they don't find me quirky and interesting. I heard Mrs. Garnett tell one of the other teachers that you were going to be running the world someday. And she wasn't saying it to make fun of you. It sounded like she hoped it would happen."

There was still something nagging at me. "I suspected you of stealing because Hazel told me you'd come into some money. Did you get an inheritance or something?"

Jasmine shook her head. "I lied to Aunt Hazel about that so she'd take Zach and me to the Algonquin Hotel for dinner," she whispered. "He was always talking about how he wanted to eat lobster but his dad would never take him. It was a really expensive meal and I used a lot of my savings. My parents were so mad when they found out. I have to wash dishes at my Uncle Avi's restaurant for the rest of the summer to earn enough to replace what I took out of the bank. I wanted him to like me so much." The idea of Jasmine washing dishes made me happy.

I sighed. I didn't know what to say. I didn't trust Jasmine and I couldn't figure out why she was being so nice to me or why she was telling me personal things. Then it hit me. Jasmine was being nice because she wanted me to keep my mouth shut about Zach. She was worried I might tell someone that she'd been head-over-heels about him and people would think less of her. "I don't plan on talking about Zach to anyone," I said.

The tension she'd been carrying in her shoulders evaporated. "Good. And I won't tell people about your detective thing. I'll make sure the Ts don't say anything, either."

We both nodded at the same time. It was a strange kind of oath we were taking, but I knew it was as binding as any promise I'd ever made.

Satisfied, she reached for the doorknob. She paused for a moment and, without turning around, said, "You know how lucky you are, right?"

"Me? How am I lucky?" I thought of all Jasmine's expensive clothes and all the people who admired her.

"You have Ralph," she said quietly. "Everyone knows you guys are best friends forever."

Before I could respond, she was out the door and running down the stairs. Maybe Jasmine's life wasn't quite as easy as I thought it was.

ᕥ ᕥ ᕥ

I watched as the Favolas' car swung left at the end of the street. Hazel dropped the arm she'd been waving wildly just a second before. As she turned to go into her house, she saw me coming down the street and waited.

"They're gone," she said.

I nodded.

"They stopped in to say good-bye and apologize one last time."

"You must be getting sick of their apologies."

Hazel stared off in the direction the car had just gone. "It's a hard thing, being in love," she mused, as much to herself as to me. Hazel was really hurt when she found out Mr. Favola had blown her off to date someone else. After that, Mr. Favola and Zach had moved to the Admiral Motel.

"I don't know about you, but I'm never falling in love," I said in my most determined voice. "Falling in like was hard enough."

Hazel smiled, but it wasn't a happy one. It was kind of sad and wistful. "Love is a funny thing," she said. "It sure can hit you hard."

"More like it can run you over, chew you up, and spit you out." I couldn't think of any more clichés, so I shut up then.

Hazel laughed. "That is the most accurate description I've ever heard. But you know, Tracy, you may change your mind someday."

I grinned. "Maybe, but my dad made me promise to stay away from boys until I'm thirty. I'm still kind of grounded, you know. This is the first time my mom has let me out by myself in a week, and even then, I have to be home in an hour."

"So I've heard," Hazel said. "Since your wings are a little clipped these days, I'm hoping your mother will let you come over and have a cup of tea with me now and then. Plus, I'm going to need some help."

"What kind of help?"

"I'm thinking about having a yard sale. I have too many things and I don't need them all. I think it's time to stop being angry and get on with life."

"I like tea," I said. We both smiled. "But don't you think me helping you with your yard sale will freak Jasmine out?"

Hazel sighed. "Maybe, but we girls have to stick together and stop tearing each other down. Besides, Jasmine likes borrowing my jewelry too much to give me ultimatums. Who knows, maybe she'll want to help? Or maybe not," she added, when she saw the skeptical look on my face.

For some reason, Hazel's goofy hair and outfit didn't seem so weird to me anymore. She was just trying to be herself, I guess, just like I was trying to be myself. It's hard when you aren't like everybody else.

I thought of Jasmine and the Ts. They sure weren't originals. But maybe they wanted to be and were too scared to try. I had some hope for Jasmine, though. The girl I was friends with in kindergarten was still in there, somewhere.

"I'm off to Brown's Store. Do you need anything?"

Hazel shook her head. "No thanks. I'm going inside, having a nice glass of lemonade, and listening to some Edith Piaf. Then I have to make a cake. Joe Tunney and his mother and sister are coming for supper tonight. It's the least I can do, considering how much Joe helped me."

Joe's name made me wince. I'd felt so humiliated when I'd begged his forgiveness. But Joe had been classy and accepted my apology. He was even saying hello when he delivered the paper again. Ralph had been right about Joe all along. It turned out Ralph had been right about a lot of things. And, best of all, Ralph and Joe were friends again.

I kind of wanted to stay and listen to Edith Piaf, since I was in a slightly sad, French singer kind of mood myself these days, but Ralph and Lester were waiting for me and I'd already burned up ten of my precious sixty minutes of freedom. I smiled and continued down the street. I'd passed a couple more houses when I heard Hazel call my name, so I turned back around.

"I forgot to tell you!" she cried. "Do you know what *Favola* means in Italian?"

I shook my head. "Bad boyfriend?"

Hazel giggled. "Nope. It means fairy tale. I thought you might like to know that."

P P P

Lester and Ralph were sitting on the bench outside of Brown's Store.

"Zach and his dad are gone," I said, taking a seat beside Lester and removing my purple sun hat. I was back wearing my hats and funky accessories. It felt good to be myself again.

Ralph said nothing, but he looked really happy. We

332

were both being a little cautious these days, working on getting things back to normal, whatever that was going to be from now on. Thank goodness Lester was around to lighten up the mood.

"Good riddance to bad rubbish!" Lester said and then took a big slurp of his Popsicle. It was so loud, Mr. Brown stuck his head out the door to see what the noise was. "Although I must say I enjoyed watching Mom tear into Zach the other night." I winced. She'd torn into me, too.

"Mom's a strong woman," he added. "Just like you, Tracy."

That made me grin. I wasn't *that* strong yet, but I would be someday. Lester didn't need to know that, though. He was convinced I was a superhero ever since I'd gotten him down from the hayloft.

"Who are you, someone's grandpa? Who says things like that anymore: *Good riddance to bad rubbish?*" I gave him a poke in the ribs and he giggled.

"I do," Lester said happily. "By the way, I'm glad you're finally here. I have this whole plan about how we can grow our detective agency."

"We don't have a detective agency," I reminded him.

Lester ignored my response and kept going. "We need flyers, word of mouth, testimonials, TV commercials, full-page ads in the newspaper—"

He stopped. His nose began to wiggle. I recognized the signs immediately and scrambled to get out of the way. And Lester being Lester, it wasn't just a single *achoo*. Instead, he began to sneeze uncontrollably, only this time Ralph was the victim of his nasal splatters. Unlike me, Ralph remained calm. He looked down at his now-glossy T-shirt, pulled Lester close, and using my brother's shirt, cleaned himself up.

Lester didn't protest. He just grinned, and as soon as Ralph was done, continued on as if nothing had happened.

"If we want to make it big, that is."

I looked at Ralph. He shook his head.

"You've got some great ideas, Lester," I said, leaning over to ruffle his unruly mop, careful to avoid the nose, "but I think our mystery-solving days are over."

"But we were just getting good at it!" Lester protested.

"We were *awful* at solving mysteries," Ralph said. "For the rest of the summer, let's just hang out and have fun."

"But you guys never want to hang out with me," Lester whined.

I looked at Ralph again. We were done being Mary Astor and Humphrey Bogart. Trixie was right: we *were* William Powell and Myrna Loy in *The Thin Man*, playing the carefree and happy Nick and Nora Charles, who never worried what people thought about them. But, of course, Nick and Nora had a sidekick: Asta, the dog.

Ralph nodded.

I stood up and looked down at Lester, who was dangerously close to dissolving into full-blown waterworks. "Lester, you've seen our secret lair, haven't you?"

"Yes . . ." Big snuffle.

"You stood up to one of the meanest guys in the history of St. Stephen, didn't you?"

"I guess so . . ." The bottom lip began to quiver.

"Look, Ralph and I are kind of used to having you hang around with us now . . ."

Lester's eyes got round and shiny. I could see the reflection of my purple hat in his irises. "Are you saying what I think you're saying?"

I nodded and gave him the one thing he wanted more than anything: "You're one of us now, Pig Face!"

THE END

(for now)

ACKNOWLEDGMENTS

So many people helped me on my journey to publication. I'll start with St. Stephen. I want to thank my childhood friends who made living on Marks Street so magical: Michael, Lisa, Alton, Johnny, Kim, Kevin, Gerald, Kathy, Arthur, Barb, and Joanne. Who you get for your parents is a lucky break; where you grow up is another. I carry every one of you with me, always. We held the keys to the kingdom for a while and I knew it even then. David Garcelon didn't blink when I told him Ralph was going to grow up to be him, which I think says a lot about what a cool, even-tempered guy he is! Thank you, as well, to the elementary school teachers who inspired me. Jane Garnett taught me in the fifth and sixth grades and graciously allowed me to use her name in this book. Decades ago, she read every story and poem I wrote (and unfortunately for her, there were lots of them) and had something kind to say about every single one. She is simply the greatest teacher I ever had. When I wondered if I could write this book, I kept telling myself "Well, Mrs. Garnett would think I could" and that was enough to keep me going. Anne McConkey and Alice McGinty: I adored you both, and your magical teaching skills have never been forgotten. Tess and Burns Getchell are in this book because how could they not be—they were like a third set of grandparents to me. So is Mr. Brown, who trusted me enough to let me go behind the counter. Evelyn Walker—you have cheered me on every step of the way, and I love you for it!

A special shout-out to Derek O'Brien, who is simply one of the loveliest people I know and threw his support behind me and the book from the get-go. Elva Hatt at the St. Stephen Public Library was also an enthusiastic supporter and is exactly the kind of librarian every town should have. Ganong Bros. Limited were kind enough to let me fangirl about their products in the book and in person and have been great supporters. I stand by Tracy that their chocolates are the best EVER.

In the dead of winter, Lisa Garcelon Blair sent me a note that said, "Can I help?" Reconnecting with her and Leanne again has been one of the greatest joys in this process. Lisa is my marketing guru. Her ideas were spot on and her excitement, humbling. I am sure that on the day of the St. Stephen launch, the two Pats, supported by Bud and Bill, will have their own party in heaven and will force a lot of people up there to read this book.

Heartfelt love to the gang: Dawn, Don, Gary, Colleen, Martine, Ron, Elaine, Denis, Mike, and Mary. You understand that good friends, good food, and the odd dance party are necessities in this life. Much love as well to Roger, Marie, Leanne, Sara, Geraldine, Ben, Joyce, Terry, and Michel, all of whom have supported me with their friendship. Love as well to my Early Childhood peeps—you are the best of the best! And Wendy Wheaton never failed to spread the word! Thanks to Anne White for always checking in and to

Elaine and Richard for being so enthusiastic! Thanks also to my blog friends who believed and to everyone who has taken the time to encourage me along the way.

I was fortunate to have wonderful critique partners: Richard Snow, Faith Knight, Mary Mesheau, and Barb Fullarton. Your advice and criticism made this book better. Thanks: to Sheree Fitch, who told me to try, to Jill Corcoran and Martha Alderson, who helped me figure out what was wrong (and right), and to Laura Backes for the early critique that kept me going. Kylie Garcelon inspired me with her own career change and wonderful storytelling. I can't wait to be an extra in one of her movies!

I bow down to my agent Lauren Keller Galit, who is fearless, cool, straightforward, and kind. You saw the potential in *Pig Face* and me and plucked us out of the slush pile. I am forever and happily in your debt. Thanks also to Caitlen Rubino-Bradway for her support, her keen eye, and inspiring talent. I think Pig Face has a crush on both of you.

Alison Weiss made me work for her, and I am glad she did. You are an amazing editor. When things got murky, Tracy and I liked to imagine you at the front of the boat holding a lantern, guiding the book home. Thanks to everyone at Sky Pony Press who worked so hard to make this a beautiful book. A special shout out for illustrator Valerio Fabrizzi—your cover brought my character to life!

A special thanks to Ben Duncan, my web designer extraordinaire, who reminds me constantly about what makes sense and what I have a budget for. Thanks to Berenice Freedome for your wonderful book trailer help! Thank you to the Sweet Sixteens and Swanky Seventeens, who have become my community and cheerleaders. When I think of you all, I hum the song "You'll Never Walk Alone" from *Carousel*. Really, I actually do. As Matt Landis would say: BOOM!

My sister Margaret always supported my writing, as has her husband Lachlan, which means a lot because they are both talented writers. A huge thanks to my brother Patrick for his enthusiasm, his music, and for the patience he's going to need for all the questions people are about to ask him. Love to my sister-in-law, Nancy Robbins, for her brain and super-reading powers.

Love to my future business manager Duncan McLeod and future world leader Daisy McLeod—you guys rock, and thanks for your help! Thanks, as well, to Joan and Warren MacKnight and Lisa MacKnight, who never fail to check in and say encouraging things.

My grandparents made me feel special; my parents made me feel loved. Their greatest gift, besides a wicked sense of humor and a belief that I could do anything, was that we lived in a world of books, and therefore, magic.

Thanks to Indy for his great company and unfailing love, even if he hogs the bed. Finally, to Barry, Sydney, and Forrest: thank you for letting me shake everything up and dream the impossible dream. You always believed, even when I did not. And you always let me drive by St. Stephen. I love you so much!